# SCAVENGER MIND WARP

Paul Stewart is a highly regarded and award-winning author of books for young readers – everything from picture books to football stories, fantasy, sci-fi and horror. His first book was published in 1988 and he has since had over fifty titles published.

Chris Riddell (Children's Laureate 2015–2017) is an accomplished artist and political cartoonist for the *Observer*. His books have won many awards, including the Kate Greenaway Medal, the Nestlé Children's Book Prize and the Red House Children's Book Award. *Goth Girl and the Ghost of a Mouse* won the Costa Children's Book Award in 2013.

Paul and Chris first met at their sons' nursery school and decided to work together (they can't remember why!). Since then their books have included the Blobheads series, The Edge Chronicles, the Muddle Earth books and Far-Flung Adventures, which include *Fergus Crane*, Gold Smarties Prize Winner, *Corby Flood* and *Hugo Pepper*, both Silver Nestlé Prize Winners.

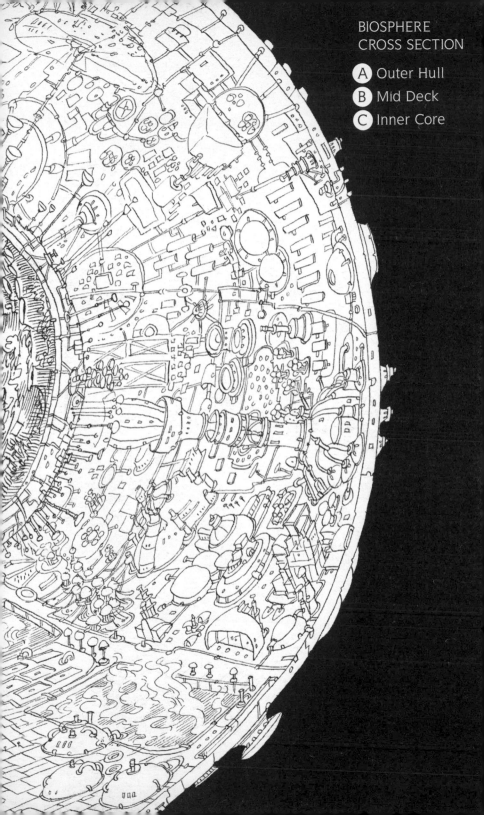

BIOSPHERE
CROSS SECTION

A Outer Hull
B Mid Deck
C Inner Core

First published 2016 by Macmillan Children's Books
an imprint of Pan Macmillan
20 New Wharf Road, London N1 9RR
Associated companies throughout the world
www.panmacmillan.com

ISBN 978-1-4472-3445-6

1 3 5 7 9 8 6 4 2

A CIP catalogue record for this book is available from
the British Library.

Printed and bound by CPI Group (UK) Ltd, Croydon CR0 4YY

For Rick

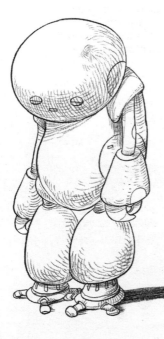

*My name is York. I'm a scavenger. I'm fourteen years old . . . I am on a mission to save mankind . . .*

These are the words I keep repeating inside my head. I have to. They're all I've got to hold on to. But it isn't easy.

I never knew the Earth first hand. All I've ever known is the Biosphere. Back in the Outer Hull I used to watch vid-streams and holo-sims of the planet we left behind. And I've walked through the Mid Deck bio-zones where deserts and rainforests and polar wastelands from Earth were recreated. I even got to swim in a man-made ocean.

But it's not the same as the real thing. It can't be. Trouble is, it's as good as it can get. The Earth died and this is all we've got left.

The Biosphere was built a thousand years ago to save everything worth saving from the dying planet. Humans, critters, eco-systems; thousands of years of wisdom and knowledge. To help it all run smoothly till we find some far-off planet to make our new home, there are also the Half-Lifes – our ancestors from the Launch Times, whose consciousness was uploaded into mind-tombs. And an army of robots.

They're the problem. The robots. Five hundred years ago, something went wrong with them. No one knows why. Not even the Half-Lifes. But the robots rebelled. They changed themselves into killer zoids, turned on humans and tried to wipe them – wipe *us* – out. A war between the two sides has been raging ever since. Zoids versus humans.

And we humans are losing.

We've always fought back as best we can. Of course we have. And for centuries we managed to hold them off. But recently things have been getting worse. Instead of killing humans, zoids in the Outer Hull have started capturing them, to find out what makes them tick. And it's tipping the war in their favour.

Like I say, I'm a scavenger, which means I get to hunt down zoids, zilch them and strip them for parts. But there's more and more of them with every day that goes by, and fewer and fewer of us. It's only a matter of time before we're wiped out completely and every trace of human existence is lost to the universe. Forever.

That's why I'm on this mission. To find out *what* went wrong. And try to put it right again.

So here I am, on my way to the centre of the Biosphere. I'm with Belle. She's a zoid, but she's not like any other zoid I've ever come across. She looks human, acts human. She's my friend. The two of us had a hard time of it in the Mid Deck. There were situations I didn't think we'd survive. But we did. Just. And now we're together, heading for the deck at the very centre of the Biosphere: the Inner Core.

The last thing I remember is the lid being closed on the black pod back in the Mid Deck. It's a container to keep our bodies alive while our minds are downloaded into the memory banks of the Biosphere's central computer. My head is spinning with everything that Belle has just told me.

'The Core is the Biosphere's brain.'

I take a moment to let that sink in. One huge computer that controls all the systems on board.

In the past it was accessed by Half-Lifes. They were the main link between the crew and the Core. But that system has broken down. Now the only way to find out what has gone wrong is to turn our own minds into digital impulses so that we can explore the memory banks for ourselves.'

Which means we'll be just like the Half-Lifes. And how will *that* feel? I wonder. But before I can ask, Belle has continued.

'The original Half-Lifes formed a part of the Core's network. It recognizes them. But it won't recognize us.'

'What do you mean?' I ask.

'I mean, York,' she says, and her eyes lock onto mine, 'we will be intruders. If the Core detects us, it will attempt to trap us in any way it can. With energy pulses, mind-warps, thought-cages, fractal mazes . . . And if it succeeds, it will erase our minds. Delete us. These pods will keep our bodies functioning, but *we* will cease to exist.'

My grip tightens on the side of the pod. The Outer Hull and Mid Deck were dangerous, but this . . . *Sluice it!* I curse under my breath. It sounds terrifying.

'So how do we avoid being detected?' I ask her.

'I will hack into the central command network and disguise our digital signatures as I guide us through the memory banks,' she says. 'I will create a thought environment that you can understand – a ladder that we'll climb down – as well as sensations you'll recognize and be able to hold on to. But remember, York,' she goes on, 'to pass undetected you must control your thoughts. Concentrate on who you are. If your mind wanders, the Core will detect us before we get a chance to enter its memory banks and find out what went wrong. It will identify us and attack us for what we are . . .'

'And what is that?' I ask.

Belle leans back and lowers the lid of the pod. Just before it clicks shut, I hear her voice:

'A virus,' she says.

We're in some kind of shaft. A massive vertical shaft that's echoey and dark and seems to have no sign of an end to it. I can't see the bottom. And I can't see the top either. I'm just going down and down and down, using this ladder that's bolted to the wall, clinging onto the rungs as tightly as I can.

My arms are aching. My hands are blistered. Leastways that's what it feels like.

But they can't be, can they? Not if it's all in my mind.

Except they can. And are. I can *see* the blisters! And my legs are shaking . . .

Hot swarf! Belle's done a good job. My body might be in the Mid Deck, but this feels so real.

I catch a glimpse of something out of the corner of my eye. A pulse of light, followed by another, and another. There's a crackle, and a fizzing ball of energy shoots past my ear. The air around me ripples in its wake.

Belle's just below me. She looks up.

'Concentrate on the ladder, York,' she says. 'One rung at a time. Don't be distracted.'

I focus on the ladder in front of me.

I hear the clunk of my heels as they come down on the rungs. I feel the coldness of the metal beneath my fingers. I lick my lips and can even taste the saltiness of sweat on my tongue.

But still I'm aware of fizzing and crackling and the background hum of the Core operating all around me. It's as though it's alive. The sounds are outside and inside me at the same time. And they're making it so difficult to concentrate.

'My name is York. I'm a scavenger,' I murmur. 'I'm fourteen years old . . .'

'That's right, York. Hold on to those thoughts,' Belle tells me. 'We need to access the memory banks before the virus scanners find us.' She pauses. 'A portal is approaching. Let go of the ladder when I give the word.'

My palms are sweating, the salt making the blisters sting as I grip the metal rungs.

'And, York,' Belle says, 'it'll be like you're in a holo-scene. But wherever you are, keep to the reality of that scene. Don't walk through walls. Or locked doors. And make sure you don't let anyone walk through *you* . . .'

Suddenly, way below me, so far down it makes me dizzy to look, there's a glow in the darkness. It gets brighter. Fast. There are rings of light, circles in circles, as pulses of energy come hurtling up towards us. For an instant everything's lit up. The shaft. The rungs. The look of concern on Belle's face.

Then it's too bright. It burns my eyes. It makes my head throb. Dazzling. Blinding. I screw my eyes shut but it makes no difference.

'Now!' Belle shouts.

I'm back in the Outer Hull. At the Inpost. Or rather, no, not *the* Inpost. Not the one I grew up in. But definitely *an* Inpost.

It's kind of familiar but different. Rooms and corridors lead off a central circle, and the air's loud with this throbbing hum.

I look round for Belle, but she's not here. And there's no one else I recognize.

The men and women I can see – and there are lots

of them – are in standard-issue kit, their kneepads and shoulder-shields gleaming in the overhead arc-lights. Some of them have protective gloves on. Others have their hoods raised, or are wearing helmets, headphones clamped to their ears.

They're all working hard. Menders are carrying out repairs to torn clothes, broken gadgets and weapons, damaged armour. A gang of four growers are plucking red berries from bushes in a grow-trough and dropping them into baskets.

No one greets me, or even looks up, as I walk between them. Then I realize why. They can't see me.

I come to a workshop area with salvagers busy dismantling scavenged zoid parts. One of them's having problems detaching the individual hub units from a urilium spine. He's grunting with effort and cursing under his breath. I see the problem at once.

The parts are from a K47 model, and with a K47 you have to work from bottom to top. He's trying to disconnect them in the wrong order.

'Not like that,' I tell him, but he can't hear me either.

I wince as his boltdriver skids and cuts into the shiny metal casing. If he's not careful, he's going to break the whole thing and leave it useless.

'Let me show you,' I say, and reach out instinctively – only to see my hand passing through his hand, and the urilium spine. Or maybe it's *his* hand passing through *mine* . . .

Whatever, I'm invisible. No one knows I'm here.

I make my way to the central Counter. Inposters on downtime are standing at the bar or seated on stools, drinking mugs of bev and satzcoa, or glasses of something fizzy. The atmosphere's happy. Rowdy even. And there in the middle of a large group is someone I do recognize.

It's Bronx!

But it's not the Bronx I know. This one is younger, his hair thicker and cropped shorter than I remember. I want to say hello, to tell him what I'm up to. But it's just not possible. When he looks my way, his gaze goes straight through me. He's telling some story or other, and

12

the men and women around him are listening carefully, sometimes frowning, sometimes smiling.

'. . . which is when I decided it was high time I made myself scarce,' he says, and shrugs, and the others explode with laughter.

I move on.

This Inpost is bigger than the one I used to call home, and nowhere near as scuzzy. The floors have been recently cleaned. The tech-sheds and mech-galleys look as though someone actually looks after them. And when I arrive at the living area, it's nothing like the cramped sleep-quarters I remember, with their skimpy sleep-pods and overflowing lockers.

There's space here. Lots of space. Enough for singles, couples and family units to live separate from one another. There are proper beds, gleaming vapour showers, cupboards and shelving, hover-sofas and recliner chairs. People are sitting, relaxing, chatting. Men, women, children. And the throbbing hum is quieter here, which means no one's having to shout.

I cross the room and pause next to a small girl who's sitting on the floor, a piece of paper in front of her. Her tongue's sticking out the side of her mouth as she concentrates on the picture she's drawing of a great big monster.

It's green and purple, with a fat rubbery body, odd-looking jointed limbs and a square head. It looks like some kind of a critter that's morphing into a zoid. Or the other way round. Then, as I watch, the girl picks up a stubby crayon and colours in the mouth and eyes bright blood red.

At the far side of the living area there's a door that leads into a small, dimly lit room. I peer inside. And there's something else I recognize in there. Two tall black casings, curved and domed, with faces shining out of them.

Half-Lifes.

One is a man with a black crew cut and a square jaw. The other is a woman with long blonde hair and laughter lines at the corners of her eyes. They're the two from my old Inpost, the ones who showed me the vid-streams from the Launch Times, and who were always there for me when I had any questions or problems.

I take a step forward, wondering if *they* can see me. But no. They don't know I'm here either.

I'm surprised by how they look and sound. Back at the Inpost, the pair of them were suffering from thought-fatigue. Their images would break up. Their voices kept crackling and fading into white noise – and even when you could make out what they were saying, the advice they gave was becoming less and less trustworthy as their minds went . . .

Then a voice comes from somewhere behind me.

'That's it, York,' it says.

I spin round and head back into the living area – and notice for the first time the young man and woman sitting on one of the hover-sofas. In the woman's arms is a baby in a pale blue playsuit. The woman's smiling as the baby feeds from the bottle of milk she's holding. The man's smiling too.

'That's it, York,' he says again as the baby slurps. 'Drink it all up. Make you big and strong, just like your daddy.'

And something inside me sort of melts. I feel like laughing and crying at the same time. It's *me* I'm looking at. With my parents. The parents I never knew properly because . . .

Right then, a siren sounds. Loud, rasping. Orange lights start flashing.

The Inpost is under attack.

Suddenly everyone's on their feet. There's running, shouting. But no panic. It's like they're going through some well-practised exercise.

'Evacuate the turbine banks!'

'Secure the Half-Lifes!'

Bronx strides into the room. 'Follow me!' he says.

He gathers everyone together and leads them back along the corridor. Someone seizes the little girl, who's clutching the picture of the monster in her hand and crying. My parents go with the rest, my mother shielding baby me as best she can.

And big me goes with them.

The Counter's packed now. Everyone's busy. Some are carrying info-pods and memory-stacks, vid-screens and holo-units. Others have boxed up the Half-Lifes and are struggling under the weight.

An evacuation's in full swing.

One man's in charge of it all. He's tall and muscular, with a white brush cut and thick grey beard, and I realize I know who he is. Seth Donahue. I've never met him before, but Bronx talked about him often enough. 'Best darned leader we ever had,' he would say, and my heart misses a beat as I remember what happened to him.

'That way,' he's urging the fleeing Inposters, his voice calm and reassuring. 'Careful with that Half-Life. Front guard, take up positions.'

Ahead of him, a group of men and women form a semicircle, and half of them drop to one knee. I recognize some of them from the workstations, but they've swapped their tools for weapons now, and at Donahue's command they start firing down a corridor on the far side of the Circle.

They're defending the Inpost, though I can't see what from. Then a huge metal figure stomps into view, and I gulp.

A killer zoid.

Like the urilium spine I saw earlier, it's a K47 model. Two legs. Arms; kitted out with laser weapons. A swivel head with sensors at the front that are vulnerable to grenbolt fire and absent in later upgrades. It lurches towards us, laser fire zinging.

And it's not alone. Another one appears behind the first. Then another. They're tooled up and returning fire, blue laser bolts criss-crossing the air.

The bev machine explodes in a shower of scalding liquid. The Counter goes up next, the marble and chrome blasted to a mess of jagged shards and molten droplets. Lights explode. Holes are zapped in walls, the ceiling . . .

And people!

They're dropping to the floor as the killers' lasers find their mark. Sisters, fathers, friends, cousins, wives . . . One after the other. There's panic now all right. The well-ordered exodus is breaking down. People are shouting, screaming, wailing as they run for cover.

Except there is no cover.

The Inpost has been overrun. The killer zoids are driving the defenders back.

Seth Donahue keeps barking commands – until he too is hit. He slams to the floor, a hole in his chest. Bronx checks him over, his lips thin as he confirms he's dead. Then he stands up straight.

'This way!' he bellows, and I swear he's aged ten

years in the last five minutes.

More killer zoids are coming in through a breach at the back of the turbine banks. Six. Seven. We're *trying to exit* through a tunnel between two mech-sheds. But there are too many people and the tunnel's too narrow. A jostling crowd has gathered, scared and muttering.

'Quick!' Bronx urges them.

Another killer zoid comes into view, lasers firing. I duck. So do my parents. But not quickly enough. And I cry out as they drop to the ground; first my father, then my mother.

It's like I'm watching it in terrible slow-mo. The shock in their faces. The way they hit the ground, then fall still. Their eyes are open, but they can no longer see. They're dead.

And I have just watched them die.

Me – baby me – I'm screaming. My face is red and scrunched up. Instinctively I reach down, try to pick myself up, but it's hopeless. I've got no substance, and my soothing coos and reassurances go unheard. Then Bronx is beside me. He stoops down and gathers the baby in his arms, and he's away, out of the turbine banks and mustering the others who are milling around outside, waiting for someone to take control now their leader's gone.

'To the convection lakes!' Bronx roars.

I watch them go, my tears turning the whole terrible scene to a misty blur. I turn away.

There's a killer zoid in front of me. And this one is different. There's some kind of holo-symbol suspended in the air above its head. A double loop, like a flattened figure eight. The symbol for infinity.

It's as if it knows I'm here.

It raises the weapon system on its arm. The lasers pivot and take aim. There's a buzzing noise. Red lights flash . . .

Then all at once it's like someone's turned up the brightness on a vid-screen. The pulses of energy are back; the blinding circles in circles.

And for a second time, I'm plunged into a total whiteout.

# 5

I'm back in the shaft.

I don't dare move, I'm shaking so badly. I just cling hold of the metal rungs. Cos that's what I have to do. Cling on. Cling on tightly.

*My name is York. I'm a scavenger. I'm fourteen years old. I am on a mission to save mankind . . .*

'York?'

It's Belle. I look down. Her green eyes seem almost to be shining in the shadowy darkness.

'That . . . that was me,' I whisper. 'As a baby. And my parents. I saw how they died. We . . .'

'I'm sorry, York,' Belle replies softly. 'I thought it would be safer for you to follow your own memory stream. But I was wrong . . .'

'My memory stream?' I say. 'But I've got no memory of what happened back then. I was too young.'

'It's in your brain, York,' she says. She reaches up and taps me on the forehead. 'Everything that ever happened to you, from the moment you were born, is stored up here. Even the things you can't access.' She pauses and I see her face cloud over. 'I . . . I'm so sorry you had to see it.'

I nod miserably. 'Where were you, Belle?' I ask her.

'I was keeping the portal open,' she says calmly. 'Maintaining pulse control. And when I sensed danger, I pulled you out. You're safe now, York. But we need to keep moving if we're going to discover why the robots rebelled,' she goes on. 'Further back into the past.'

I swallow. It's not going to be easy. But I know she's right.

'OK,' I tell her.

We head deeper and deeper down into the shaft that Belle has created to help me make sense of this extraordinary place – a mind-ladder that I cling to. There are columns of flickering green lights and electro-static flashes. Fractals glimmer. Synaptic connections fizz and spark.

I focus on the ladder – the glint of the metal, the *clunk-clunk* of my boots on the rungs.

We keep on. I try to stay focused, but I'm finding it more and more difficult to concentrate. I can't stop thinking about the Inpost in the turbine banks. Of Seth Donahue. And Bronx. And of my parents – alive, then dead . . .

I hear something.

It's like a soft cry, echoing far in the distance. I pause,

look around me. But there's nothing there. I'm about to
continue down the rungs of the ladder when suddenly
the noise grows loud. Deafeningly loud.

It's a deep, throaty, savage, blood-curdling roar, and
it's coming from right behind me. I turn, and there, deep
inside the pulsing darkness, I see something forming . . .

'Concentrate on the ladder, York,' Belle tells me
urgently.

But it's already too late.

A rubbery green-and-purple body flops and sloshes as it floats through the air towards me, red eyes blazing. It's grotesque, but also looks ridiculous. Like some kind of cartoon. Or toy. But horribly menacing. Hinged limbs extend and retract. A square head rotates, the fanged mouth gaping wide as the roaring sound grows so loud I can feel it trembling through my body, pounding inside my head.

Then it's on me. Warm. Stifling. Wrapping itself around me, swallowing me up.

I try to move but cannot. The monster or whatever it is tightens its grip. It's squeezing the air from my lungs. It's crushing my bones. I want to cry out, but when I open my mouth the soft rubbery stuff it's made of oozes in and I can't spit it out. I can't make a sound. And I can't breathe . . .

*Belle! Belle!* my thoughts scream.

My eyes are clamped open. The purple and green of the monstrous body seem to glow. The blood red glints in its wicked-looking eyes.

And suddenly, it's like I can *feel* the colour.

The purple hurts like bruises, till my whole body's throbbing with the pain of a bad beating. The green is sickly and sour and makes me want to throw up. And the *red* . . .

Sharp. Intense. Blistering hot. It burns my eyes and brands my skin. It brings my blood to the boil . . .

Belle! Help me, Belle . . . *Belle!*

'Hold on,' I hear her calling back at last. 'Just keep holding on to what you know, York . . .'

*York.*

I do what she tells me.

*My name is York. I'm a scavenger. I'm fourteen years old. I'm on a mission to save mankind. My body is lying in a pod in the Mid Deck . . . My name is York . . .*

I grip the rungs of the ladder tight as I can. Mustn't let go. Mustn't fall.

Just have to . . . hold . . . on . . .

The rubbery stuff in my mouth melts away. My eyes clear. And I see Belle.

She's above me, reaching out, her hands clamped around two of the monster's angular limbs. It's howling, its multicoloured body quivering and writhing as it tries to break away. But Belle doesn't let go. And as she continues to hold on tightly, I see something start to happen.

The colours shift. The throbbing purple drains out of its body, down into Belle's arms, and is gone; the green fades; the spots of red shrink – until I'm looking through this formless transparent shape that cracks and breaks up, loses substance and drifts away like flakes of nothing.

And I'm all right.

I don't hurt any more. I don't feel sick. I'm in the shaft, holding onto the rungs of the mind-ladder.

'What was *that*?' I ask Belle.

She reaches up and taps me on the forehead again. 'Something from in here,' she says.

'So I imagined it . . .'

And then it hits me. It was the little girl's drawing that I saw in the Inpost. I tell Belle.

She nods. 'It was a mind-warp, York. You let your thoughts wander. The Core's virus scanners picked up on it and took one of your memories – a harmless little memory – and warped it into something to use against you . . .'

As she's speaking I notice that there's a glow beginning far down in the shaft once more. It gets brighter and brighter. Concentric circles and pulses of energy. A ring of spiralling light that comes speeding up towards me.

Hot swarf! It's happening again!

'Prepare to let go,' I hear Belle calling.

My head buzzes with light, outside, inside . . .

'*Now!*'

I'm standing on a high walkway, up near hot, dazzling arc-lights. Below me is a tech-scape I recognize. There are flux-towers and power-pylons, a tube-forest and circuit-board plains. Far in the distance, coils of grey mist hover over the acid lakes.

I'm back in the Outer Hull. Sometime in the past.

*My name is York . . .*

There's a group of figures directly below me. Seven of them. Three men, four women. And they're in trouble. Crouched down behind a sump tank, they're looking over their shoulders, checking all round them. They look frightened . . .

'Give yourselves up.'

The voice is a mechanical monotone. It's coming from somewhere behind a bunch of transistor stacks. It sounds like some kind of killer zoid. But when it plods into view, it doesn't look like any killer zoid I've ever seen.

'Give yourselves up.'

The killer zoids I'm used to are monstrous machines, designed to cause max damage. They've got cutters

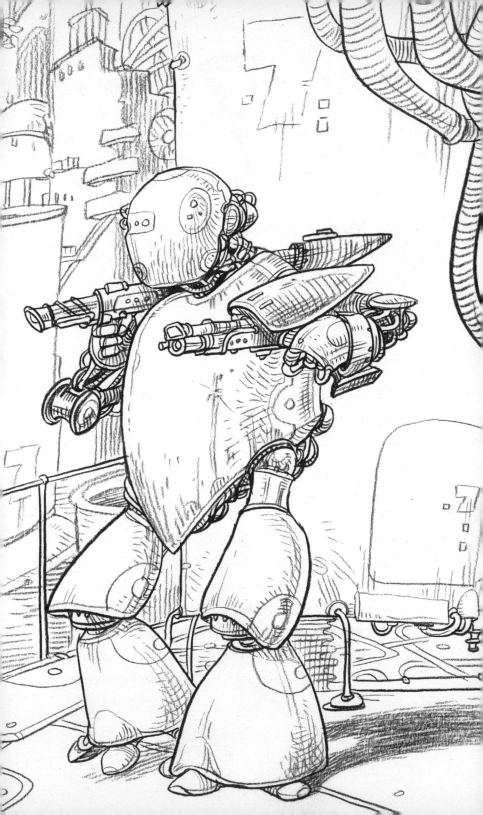

or lasers rather than hands; roller treads or pneumatic pistons for legs; and there isn't the least trace of a recognizable face on any of their upper units. This one though, it looks kind of human. It's got arms and legs, a barrel-shaped body and a round head, with blinking eye sensors. And its weapons are carried, not built into its body. Though they look just as deadly.

'Give yourselves up.' The laser trembles in its grasp. 'Do not resist.'

And it's speaking. Later models did not speak. This one must be a really early zoid upgrade.

'Do not resist,' it drones again, and, as the humans panic and break cover, it swings round and fires the laser.

The sump tank explodes in a shower of flaming gloop. The humans run. The killer zoid fires again, with a pulser this time, strafing the air with molten grenbolts.

There's a cry, and the air fills with the stench of scorched flesh. One man stumbles and falls. Then one of the women – and then another. The others split up and fan out, and try to take cover where they can.

'Destroy.' The killer zoid's voice is flat and emotionless. 'Destroy. Destroy.'

I race past it. I'm not sure what to do, but I want to be with the other humans. To listen to what they're saying. To find out where I am and what's going on.

We lose the lumbering zoid, and I catch up with

the four of them on the far side of a large box-shaped generator unit. They've regrouped and are hunkered down on the ground, deep in conversation. I read the name patches sewn onto their tunics.

*Dirk Miller. Sam Burgess.*
*Tonya Jenkins. Alice Kett.*

Ordinary names. Ordinary people. Humans, just like me.

'We've got to go back for them,' Alice is saying. She sounds close to tears.

'We can't,' Dirk insists.

'But Lyla and Sarita . . . And Rufus . . .' she protests. 'We can't just leave them there.'

'There's nothing we can do for them now,' says Sam grimly.

I realize I'm nodding. Their three friends are dead. What the rest of them need to do now is start making plans. To zilch the zoid. To get to somewhere safe. But Alice Kett is howling.

'Rufus . . . Oh, *Rufus* . . .'

Sam hushes her angrily. 'Do you want to get all of us killed too?' he hisses.

Too right! I think.

'We need to think about our next move,' says Dirk.

At least one of them's got some sense.

But it's soon pretty clear they're all a bit clueless, and it occurs to me that these are not scavengers. They're scientists, trained to maintain the Biosphere, not deal with zoids that are out to kill them. They've got soft hands, they're unarmed, and they don't seem to have any understanding of just how much danger they're in.

Dirk looks at his wrist-scanner. I notice the date.

*Time – 21:09:44. Year – LY501.*

'Launch Year five hundred and one,' I breathe.

That's why the killer zoids look so old-fashioned. That's why the humans are so useless at dealing with them. I'm witnessing the start of the robot rebellion, five hundred years after the Launch Times. And these humans in front of me don't have the first idea what's going on.

'But *why* is this happening?' Tonya Jenkins is saying, her ponytail swishing back and forth as she looks from one of her friends to the other.

'Yeah, what's gone wrong with the robots?' asks Sam Burgess.

'Just some little glitch,' says Dirk Miller. 'The techies are working on it.' He reaches out and pats Sam on the back. 'They'll soon get it sorted.'

*No! No! No! No! No!* I want to shout.

They won't get it sorted. They can't. This isn't a little glitch. It's a basic malfunctioning of the primary robotic protocol. Instead of serving and protecting human beings as they were programmed to do, they're out to kill humans. Each and every one of us. The four scientists don't know this.

And there's no way I can tell them.

Luckily, Dirk Miller seems to be taking control.

'We need to arm ourselves,' he's saying. 'That robot's got weapons.'

'But . . .' the others protest.

He raises a hand to silence their objections, then climbs to his feet. And as I watch, he unscrews the side panel of the generator unit, turns off the power supply and unravels a length of the cable inside. Using a small pocket knife, he strips the cable of its outer casing, loops it into a noose, then lays it on the ground. He pulls a small interspeak from his top pocket and activates it.

*Beep! Beep! Beep! Beep!*

Clever, I think.

He places it on the ground at the centre of the broad circle of bare wires. Then, taking the end of the cable, he switches the power supply back on and climbs up onto the top of the generator.

The killer zoid has already responded to the beeping. Like I said, it's an early upgrade. It can't track human heat-sigs. But it can use its tracker device to zone in on any piece of tech that humans might be carrying. Digi-comps and B-phones. Interspeaks . . .

'Destroy! Destroy! Destroy!' It's getting closer.

Dirk Miller stays cool. While the others hide themselves behind nearby pulse-stacks and capacitor drums, he crouches down on the roof of the generator unit. And waits.

Moments later, the zoid lurches into view. Its visual sensors are flashing like two red eyes.

'Destroy. Destroy.'

It homes in on the interspeak. Dirk peers down over the edge of the generator roof, watching intently as the zoid steps inside the circle of stripped cable, then pauses. There's a trill of twiddly bleeps as it computes what it has found.

And suddenly Dirk Miller's straightening up and tugging hard on the insulated end of the cable. The noose of bare wire closes up round the zoid's legs – sending five hundred thousand volts through its metal body.

'Destr . . .
*iiiiiiiiiiiiiii . . .*'

The zoid's mechanical screech is loud and piercing. Its weapons drop to the ground. White smoke spurts from every riveted joint. Sparks fly. Zoid-juice hisses and spits. The metal panels of its chest and head start to glow; red, then yellow, then white. The screeching gets louder, until . . .

There's a colossal *BANG!* as the killer zoid explodes. Scraps of wiring and splinters of metal fly in all directions.

Dirk Miller drops the cable and jumps down from the top of the generator unit to inspect the damage. The others join him, congratulate him, pat him on the back.

'Two lasers, two pulsers,' he announces, as he hands out the weapons the killer zoid was carrying.

'And I reckon we ought to salvage that motherboard,' says Sam Burgess. 'The binary codes of the data-chip might give the techies some clue about what's going on.'

'And what about the urilium leg units?' Tonya Jenkins suggests. 'And the back panel. They could probably be turned into some kind of armour . . .'

I smile to myself. I'm face to face with the Biosphere's first scavengers.

I travel with the four of them as they head off.

This holographic record of the past is fascinating, and so real. But I mustn't forget why I'm here. To find out what turned the robots against humanity in the first place. At any moment the virus scanners might detect me. I can only hope Belle is ready to pull me back to the mind-ladder.

The group make their way across a broad plain, dotted with energy domes, glowing power cables streaked between them. I look up to see a collection of bulbous-looking buildings towering high above the ground, and raised walkways, crowded with people.

The dead havens!

I recognize this place. I've been here before. Back in the Outer Hull when I was trying to find Sector 17. It was where I first met Belle.

Except it's not dead now. I'm seeing the buildings as they were designed to be – living quarters for the crew members who live in the Outer Hull.

We come to a perimeter fence that's humming with

some kind of force-field. It looks new and hastily put together. Dirk presses his hand to a security sensor set into a gateway. There's a buzz, and a steel door swings open. We step into the compound.

Approaching the buildings, I notice the pools set into the black marble at the base of the pillars. Some have fountains and mini-waterfalls, reeds and pondweed, and silver and gold fish that are darting about in the water. Others – larger and lined with turquoise-blue tiles – have been designed for downtime swimming. For humans. Not that there's anyone swimming in them right now.

As we walk closer, the shutters of one of the overhead cabins fly open and a head appears. 'You're back!' a voice shouts down. 'What's it like out there?'

'Not good,' Dirk Miller calls back.

'They shot down Lyla, Sarita and Rufus,' Tonya blurts out, which sets Alice Kett off crying again.

Sam puts an arm around her shoulder, and the four of them – with me following close behind – take one of the walkways up to the aerial cabins. When we reach the platform at the top we're confronted by a group of men, women and children. They're all talking at once.

'What's going on?'

'What's wrong with the robots?'

'What are we going to do?'

A woman, her arms wrapped around her little son and daughter, looks as if she's about to cry. 'How bad *is* it?' she asks bleakly.

Dirk Miller breathes in deep. 'Bad,' he says. 'The robots have armed themselves. They've taken control of the convection lakes, the admin block and viewing deck—'

'The Central Robot Hub,' Sam Burgess butts in. 'They're ransacking the spare parts there. Upgrading themselves.'

'And they've jammed all communication with the Mid

Deck and Inner Core,' adds Tonya Jenkins. 'We're on our own.'

'The good news though is that they're not indestructible,' Dirk says, and grins as he holds up his laser.

One of the haven-dwellers nods. 'We've been doing our bit here as well,' he says. 'Some of us broke into the emergency armoury. Kitted ourselves up with weapons and ammo in case the robots attack.'

'It's going to take more than a couple of lasers to defend ourselves against the zoids,' says Alice bleakly.

'Zoids?' someone says.

'It's Sam's name for them,' Dirk explains. 'On account of the noise their weapons make when they're powering up.'

Hot swarf, I think. So *that's* why they're called zoids. I've often wondered.

Whatever, it's like the zoids have heard him, cos at that exact moment there's a low buzzing noise from all along the perimeter fence. Then a series of explosions. I spin round to see long sections of the wire fizz and spark; then collapse.

With the force-field down, the killer zoids tramp into the compound. There's a small army of them.

All at once, the arc-lights go out. There are bumps and muffled crashes from inside the havens. Someone calls out. Someone else screams.

The zoids start firing and the air is suddenly bright with lines of laser light and the white and yellow flashes of flame. Visiglass windows smash and holes appear in walls. Great chunks of red-hot metal break off and come crashing down to the ground below, or splash into the pools, where they hiss and send up clouds of billowing steam.

The haven-dwellers fight back with laser weapons and grenbolt pulsers. Orange tracer fire zings past my ears. Laser bolts blind me.

I'm in the middle of a full-scale battle.

Adults form a circle around the children and retreat,

shooting back at the zoids as they go.

As I look down from the platform, one zoid steps on a marked paving stone, and there's a deafening explosion as the mine beneath it goes off and hurls it up into the air. Zoid-juice showers down and I breathe in the stench of melted circuitry.

But the zoids keep coming. And – sluice it! – there are masses of them. Far too many to hold back . . .

Then something changes.

Zoids are beginning to fall. One after the other. They're being zilched. From behind. I see one zoid get hit square in its back panel by a grenbolt and slam to the ground. Another keels over as its head unit explodes. Then another. And another. A band of armed men and women are coming in across the power-plains, their weapons blazing, knocking out as many of the attacking zoids as possible before they can return fire.

'Go on,' I urge the counter-attackers excitedly.

With the zoids distracted, the people of the havens stream down the walkways, uncover air ducts and drainage pipes and disappear underground. The armed band of men and women hold off the zoids for as long as they can, then follow the last of the fleeing survivors. I hear the clang of the metal covers as they slam shut.

And I realize that what I've witnessed now is the beginning of humans taking refuge in secret hideouts.

The first of
the Inposts.
The clank and
hum of the departing
zoids interrupts my thoughts. The
havens – the *dead* havens – are
deserted.

I head back through the cabins, taking
one walkway, then another, picking my way over
abandoned bits and pieces that are strewn across the
floors. A toy critter with blue fur and a long neck;
smashed pictographs and half-packed backcans; a bev-
mug, its handle broken off and a jagged crack passing
through the red painted heart on its side . . .

*Click . . . Whirr . . .*

I stop in my tracks, spin round. Not all the zoids have
left. There's one behind me, eyes flashing and laser

raised. I recognize the holo-symbol with the flattened figure of eight pulsing in the air above its head.

My heart quickens. The virus scanner has detected me for a second time. I've got to get out of here. And fast.

'Belle,' I murmur. 'Belle, where are you?'

I retreat slowly, one step after the other. I'm waiting for the rings of energy, for the blinding circles in circles. The whiteout.

But that's not what happens.

As I watch, the zoid raises an arm. Tendrils of light sprout from its fingers and spread through the air, creating a glowing web around me. The zoid pulls back its arm and the scene I've been reliving is torn away like a curtain, leaving me hovering in blackness.

I reach out. My fingers touch a face, a human face.

Lips, nose, forehead . . . And hair. Short hair.

I snatch my hand away.

'Who are you?' I whisper.

'Who are you? Who are you? Who are you?'

The words – *my* words – echo around me in a mesmerizing ripple. And it isn't just my *words* that I can hear. It's my *voice* too.

I swallow anxiously.

'Where am I?' I ask.

'Where am I? Where am I? Where am I?'

My words again. My voice. Multiplied a thousand times as a loud chorus that fills the air.

Slowly my eyes are beginning to adjust to the darkness. Shapes emerge. Figures. I'm standing in the middle of a great crowd that sways from side to side and shuffles back and forth.

I attempt to make my way through the mass of people, but they close in tightly around me and press me back. They bear down on me, suffocating me. They push. They jostle. They keep me standing where I am.

I cannot get away.

I realize there's no point in trying, and give up. I stare back at them – and find myself face to face with . . . with myself.

There are thousands of me. Image after image. It's like looking in a shattered mirror.

A cold panic rises inside me. And as it does so, the pressure of the bodies crowding in on me increases.

'Get away!' I shout, and again a thousand voices shout back at me.

'Get away! Get away! Get away!'

But they do not move. There is no escape. I'm trapped.

Trapped by myself; by the countless reflections of myself who will not let me go. And there is absolutely nothing that I can do about it. When I push, the crowd pushes back. When I cry out, my voice comes back at me, echoing my own rising terror.

Suddenly I'm flailing wildly, desperate to escape. But only for a moment. It's hopeless. The more I fight against them, the more they press in. I know that if I struggle, then I will be crushed.

This is not the way, I tell myself.

I stop resisting. The pressure around me eases at once. Fighting back the blind panic, I still my thoughts and clear my head. And slowly, slowly, I allow myself to let go.

This is the opposite of what Belle's been telling me to do. I realize that. *Hold on*; that's what she's kept on telling me. *To your name, to your age, to who you are. To the mission . . .*

But now in my mind I evaporate, becoming as insubstantial as a cloud of mist. And after that, instead of trying to force my body through the crowd, I begin to seep between them, slipping past countless reproductions of myself. I move softly, silently, almost unseen . . .

Far in the distance, a pulsing light appears. It grows brighter and I move towards it, not allowing myself to think of what is happening, what I'm doing. The light grows brighter, brighter . . .

And I'm suddenly released from myself.

I'm back in the memory banks.

Whatever just happened, it's over. But while it was going on, I reckon it was just about the weirdest, most frightening thing I've ever experienced. Like a nightmare. But worse, because I couldn't wake up from it.

It was like I'd turned against myself. Belle told me all about the dangers of mind-warps and thought-cages and fractal mazes. But after what I've just been through, it seems like the greatest danger I'm ever going to have to face . . . is *me*.

Looking round, I find that I'm standing in a low-ceilinged room with tinted visiglass windows, all of them cracked or broken. It's a huge computer hub. Head-high walls split the hall up into dozens of separate pods, each one complete with terminals, decks and holo-screens. I guess that once, not so long ago, the place was buzzing with activity as tech-operatives worked together to keep the Outer Hull running smoothly.

Not now.

The machines are still humming, but there's no one at

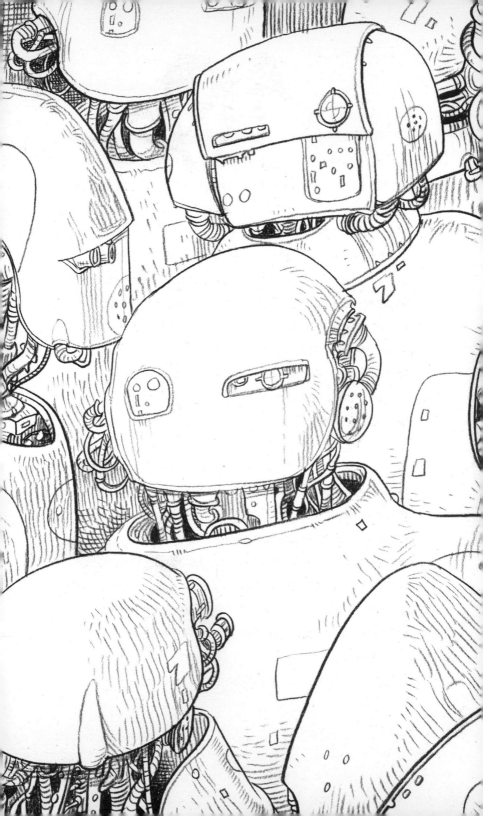

the info-decks, no one monitoring the flickering screens. It's like every single person's just upped and left.

The thing is though, the hall is not empty. Instead of people, there are zoids here. Lots of them. I look round hurriedly to check whether any of them has the infinity symbol hovering over its head.

All clear.

The zoids are carrying out tasks I can't guess at. They're communicating with one another, their eyes flashing red, first one, then another in silent response.

It's weird and spooky seeing this scene of zoids evolving into machines that are independent of humans. I'm guessing that this must be the moment when, having turned from helpers to killers, they began to form themselves into an army.

My stomach's churning. My head's in a whirl.

I pass through a second doorway.

'Hot swarf!' I exclaim.

I'm standing in a place that's been designed by and for zoids, not for humans at all. There are no desk-pods. No workstations. No overhead lights. Apart from the red, green and blue dials glowing at a thousand display panels, and the twinkling white pulses of energy moving endlessly along a tangle of cables that criss-cross the air from floor to ceiling, the place is in darkness. And then I see them.

Humans. Twenty of them, maybe more. Men and women.

Some are sitting, heads bowed and slumped forward, or hugging their knees and rocking slowly back and forth. Others are lying motionless on the floor. Their eyes are all open, but they're glazed and unseeing. Strands of glistening drool hang from the corners of their open mouths. They're bone thin, with matt grey skin.

They look . . . empty.

A man is strapped into a chair. Curved bands of urilium at his wrists, ankles and neck are holding him in place. He looks terrified.

Sections of motherboard, lengths of cable and struts of hardware surround the chair. And, as I watch, a dome-shaped helmet, with wires and cables coming out of it, descends and covers the man's head. There's a buzzing sound, and zigzags of dazzling static zing across from the metal helmet to the man's head. Beneath it, his body twitches and convulses.

When the helmet rises again, the man slumps forward. His terror has gone, but no other emotion has taken its place. He looks just like Gaffer Jed, Lina's grandfather, did after his thoughts and memories were uploaded into the death zoid back in the Outer Hull. Empty. Drained.

But what's happened to *this* man's thoughts and memories?

'Hold on.'

The voice is distant.

'York, hold on.'

*York.*

'Hold on to what you know,' she's telling me.

*My name is York . . . I'm a scavenger . . .*

And as I say the words, circles of white light appear in front of me. They grow brighter and brighter. I step forward into them . . .

And I'm back in the shaft again.

My body shakes violently as I grip the mind-ladder. The darkness around us is pulsing and the air is thick with billowing cloud. Belle's standing just below me. When she speaks, her voice is accompanied by flashes of light and a strange echoing hiss.

I concentrate on her words.

'Are you all right?' she's asking me.

'I am now,' I say. 'It . . . it was like I travelled back in time, Belle,' I tell her. 'To five hundred years after the Launch Times, just after the robot rebellion. I was in the Outer Hull . . .'

Belle's nodding.

'But then a virus scanner caught me. It was disguised as a zoid. I found myself in this weird place, surrounded by a massive crowd of . . . of myself. Thousands of me. I panicked. But then I sort of, I don't know . . . kind of let my thoughts go . . .'

'You did well, York,' she says, and I'm pleased to hear the approval in her voice. 'You were trapped inside a thought-cage.'

'*That* was a thought-cage?' I say numbly.

She nods. 'I was afraid I'd lost you, York. And I don't know what I'd have done if I had.' She turns away, but not before I've seen the look of pain in her face. 'Luckily,' she goes on, 'I picked up your thought-signature at a synaptic junction back there and managed to open the portal. But we might not be so lucky next time. The virus scanners are getting close, so we're going to have to move faster.'

'What exactly are we looking for, Belle?' I ask her. 'I've witnessed the destruction of living quarters, the fightback by the crew, zoids uploading humans' minds—'

'That is the trail we need to follow,' Belle interrupts. 'We must find the moment when the first robot rebelled against its primary protocol and harmed a human. I have detected a neural pathway at Launch Year 500 which looks promising.'

Just then, the shaft suddenly brightens. Concentric rings of dazzling light rise up from the shadowy depths below. I grip the rungs of the mind-ladder.

Belle's voice sounds in my ear. 'Let go, York. And take care . . .'

Once more I look around me, trying to get my bearings. I'm standing in some kind of storage depot. In front of me are rows of low sheds, twenty or so in all, each one with a sign on its door. *PH Mark I – Head Units. PH Mark II – Head Units. PH Mark IV – Limb Units*. And so on. Robot parts. Behind me is a vast hangar. On one of its double doors is a sign that looks more promising.

*PH Mark I – Assembled Units.*

I'm about to go inside when I hear voices behind me, and I turn to see two people coming towards me. Two men. Like the ones I saw earlier, their names are on patches stitched to their tunics. *Pat Hinton. Jackson Chung*. They're sharing some kind of a joke, roaring with laughter.

'Next thing I know, it collapses,' says Pat.

'So what did you say?' Jackson chuckles.

Pat grins. 'You don't want to know,' he tells him, then adds. 'But it wasn't polite.'

And the pair of them roar with laughter all over again.

I smile to myself. Back in the Inpost where I grew up

there wasn't much laughter. We were under constant attack. Life was grim and people were serious. Not like these two, who are relaxed, happy and seemingly without a care in the world. I envy them.

Jackson is carrying a large tool bag. Pat is holding a heavy metal wrench in one hand and has what looks like a holo-pad tucked under his other arm.

'Come on then,' says Jackson, slapping his friend on the back. 'Let's get this thing done.'

They enter the hangar. I follow them.

Belle is back on the mind-ladder, keeping the portal open with her thoughts. Pulse control, as she calls it. I've just got to trust her to pull me out if things go wrong.

Inside, the place is cavernous and dark. We head down the central aisle past crates, barrels and stacks of sheet metal. As the two men walk forward, lights come on overhead, illuminating the gloom below. They come to a halt. Pat runs a finger down the holo-pad he's holding, then looks up and points.

'They should be over there,' he says, and the pair of them stride over to the far corner.

Behind a screen is a line of robots. They look familiar. They're friendly-looking machines. Squat, round and with stubby legs and arms, they have two eyes and a mouth that's fixed in a welcoming smile. I find myself smiling back.

Ralph!

Robotic-Assist Level Personal Help. One of these units once saved my life. Back in the Clan-Safe it was, when that madman Dale was trying to have me killed. It died – if 'died' is the right word for a robot – in the process. But

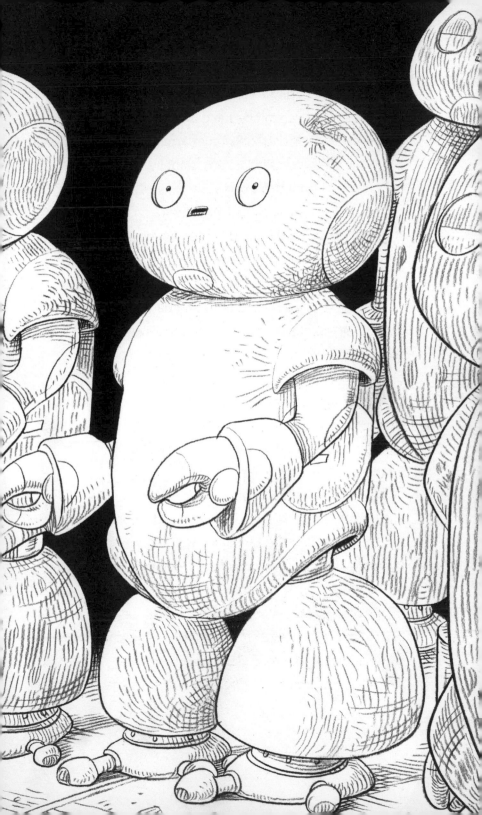

I kept hold of the simple data memory-chip embedded in the interface unit that carried its consciousness. I remember slipping it into the pocket of my flakcoat.

'Any idea why this lot were decommissioned?' Pat is asking his friend.

'Better upgrades made them obsolete, I suppose,' Jackson says, setting his tool bag down on the floor. 'But Casey reckons they can be stripped for parts.'

Pat walks up to one of the robots and peers into its dark visiglass eyes. It's got a long scratch down the left

side of its head, and a small dent.

'Reckon it'll still work?' asks Jackson.

Pat inspects the notes on his holo-pad again. 'It says here that a Mark 1 Personal Help unit is activated by pressing a button at the back of its neck.'

'I reckon this Mark probably needs recharging,' says Jackson.

Pat nods. 'Probably,' he says. 'But I'll give it a go.'

With the wrench still gripped in one hand, he reaches round the back of the robot. There is a click, followed by a hum, and the robot's eyes glow red.

'Wow,' Jackson breathes, impressed. 'After all this time . . .'

'Greetwell,' the robot says. Its voice is soft and warm, but there's something sinister in his tone that makes my flesh crawl. It scans the name patches. 'Greetwell, Pat Hinton and Jackson Chung. How may I serve you?'

The two men look at one another and laugh. 'Give us a little dance,' says Pat.

The robot tries its best, swaying from side to side, its stubby arms waving about. The men think this is hilarious.

'How about a cartwheel?' says Jackson.

The robot pauses. 'A cartwheel?' it repeats. 'I am afraid I do not understand the meaning of this term.'

Which makes them laugh all the louder.

'Well, if you can't do cartwheels,' says Pat, 'I'm afraid you're no use to us. Stripping for parts it is,' he adds, and reaches behind the robot's neck again to switch it off.

The robot lurches back. 'Perhaps I can assist in another way,' it says in that same creepy voice.

And as it speaks, the glowing eyes change. The two discs of red light become a pair of bright yellow dots at the centre of a circle of black. Then suddenly, and without any warning, it reaches out and seizes the wrench from Pat's hand.

'Woah! What's going on?' Pat says. 'I—'

The wrench comes down hard on the top of his head. Pat collapses in a heap.

Jackson is frozen with shock, unable to believe what he is seeing. The wrench slams down a second time, and he slumps to the floor beside his friend.

The robot turns to the next one in the line. It reaches up behind its neck and activates it. Then, standing in front of the second robot, it raises an arm and presses the chest panel. There's a fizzing crackle between them, and the second robot's glowing eyes change, also becoming two hard yellow dots. The robot has communicated something. Something bad. And as I stand there, transfixed, all along the line robot after robot is activated and turned into a killer.

'Belle! Belle!' I whisper urgently. 'Get me out of here!'

The concentric rings of dazzling white light appear at my feet, and I step into them.

# 13

'So we now know what model of robot first rebelled,'
Belle says when I describe what I've just witnessed. 'It's
a start. The next step is to track that first bad Ralph unit
back in time through the memory banks. But with more
than five hundred years to search through, it's not going
to be easy . . .'

She notices I'm shaking my head. 'What is it, York?'
she says.

'Not Ralph,' I say. 'I can't call that thing back there
"Ralph". Ralph saved my life. Ralph was good. The robot
I just saw back there was evil. It killed two men—'

'All right,' says Belle, cutting me short. 'So what do
you want to call it?'

'I'm not sure. I . . .' And then I remember the name
Jackson Chung gave it. 'Mark,' I say.

'Mark,' Belle repeats.

'For Mark 1,' I explain.

She nods. 'Of course. From now on, I shall refer to the
bad Ralph unit as Mark. I shan't forget.'

'Thanks,' I say, and suddenly feel stupid for making a

fuss over the name of a robot. 'It would be like if it was called Belle,' I tell her. 'Do you understand?'

Belle goes silent. She's thinking.

'You would not like it to be called Belle because you do not like *it*, but you do like *me*,' she says at last, each word spoken slowly and precisely. She tilts her head to one side. 'When you heard the name, you wouldn't know how to feel.'

And I laugh. 'That's exactly it,' I tell her.

'I understand,' she says.

She's learned something new. Belle is always learning, and becoming more and more like a human as she does so. But just as I'm about to point that out to her, her expression becomes serious.

'We need to find the moment when Mark's primary protocol was altered,' she says. 'And why. If it was in that storage location in Launch Year 500 . . .'

She pauses as she downloads data from the black pod where our bodies, our actual bodies, are lying, rather than these virtual bodies that she has created for my benefit here in the Core.

'There were still a few units active as late as Launch Year 293,' she says. 'Prepare to step through the portal when I locate the synaptic junction . . .'

I grip the mind-ladder and wait for the white-out. It swallows me up. When the light fades I'm back in the memory banks.

I'm on a raised walkway that overlooks a vast atrium. It's another part of the Outer Hull I've been to before. An admin sector with the viewing deck up at the top. There is a visiglass elevator in front of me. I step into it.

Belle has warned me to keep to the reality of the holographic scenes I enter. I could walk through walls or closed doors, or float across open spaces, she tells me. But this would create ripples, disjoints in the digital flow. And that's exactly what the virus scanners are looking out for. There's no sign of them for now.

Unfortunately there's no sign of the bad Mark robot either. But I keep looking.

The elevator speeds me down to the ground floor of the vast admin block. I find myself looking at a sign etched into one of the side panels.

*COMMON OAK (Quercus robur)*
*Seedling planted: Launch Time, Year Zero*

There, on the other side of the visiglass at the centre of the atrium is the oak tree. Standing in its dome-shaped grow-trough, it is nearly three hundred years old, and in its prime. It's good to see it again. I last saw it back in the

Outer Hull seven hundred years in the future, still going strong.

The elevator glides to a halt. I step out and look around me. The atrium is full of people. Scientists. Technicians. Bio-engineers. Moving between them are robots. Hundreds of them, and all of them sleeker and more high-tech than bad Mark. There's a determined optimism in the faces of the people as they and their robot helpers carry out their work. I'm overwhelmed with a feeling of terrible sadness that all this is doomed to go so horribly wrong.

Belle and I must find out what triggered the robot rebellion.

For now, they all seem fine. As I leave the admin block and head off into the Outer Hull, I see more robots. Loads of them. Everywhere. They're working on their own and in groups – monitoring the ventilation pipes, energy feeds and waste sluices of the tube-forest; maintaining the radiation pylons and cooling chimneys; transporting rubbish skips to the acid lakes.

It's a wonderful scene. Humans and robots working together for the good of the Biosphere . . .

'Descale the cold-water inflow unit,' a wiry-looking man in a white boiler suit is instructing a tall, streamlined robot with articulated hand units.

The two of them are standing at the base of a tall

oxy-hydro converter. A jet of steam is hissing out from an upper valve – too much steam, judging by the look of concern on the man's face, and by the orange warning light that's flashing on the control panel.

'At once, sir,' the robot responds. It glides towards the converter, arms outstretched and eyes flashing red. 'My role is to serve.'

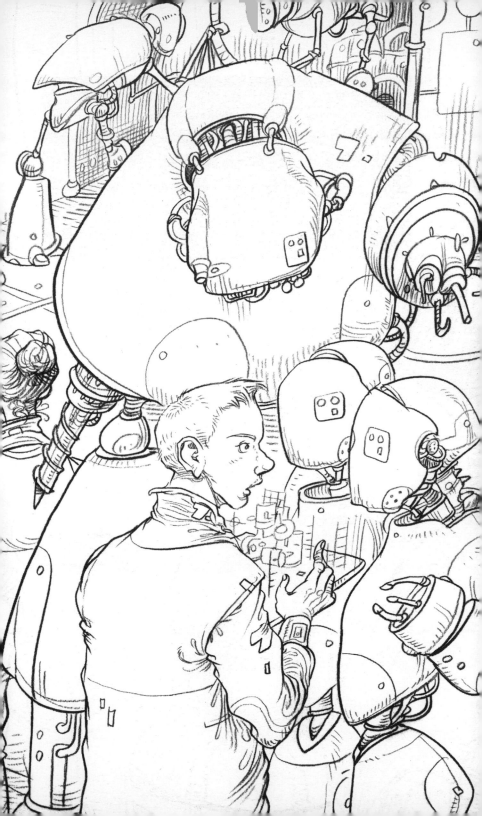

As I watch, the robot leans forward and checks the front panel. Then, using a boltdriver, it removes the inspection cover. There's a loud glugging noise and, high above, the pressure of the steam increases. The air fills with a piercing high-pitched whistle. The orange warning light turns red.

'Additional robotic assistance requested, sir,' the robot says calmly, its metal head swivelling around to the man, who taps at a holo-pad.

'Additional robotic assistance confirmed,' he says.

Two more robots arrive. One is carrying a large box of tools. The other has a coiled length of tubing over one shoulder. The man turns away and, communicating between themselves with bleeps and flashing lights, the three robots work together to fix the fault.

Minutes later, it's done. The steam has stopped hissing. The light becomes a constant green.

I'm feeling uneasy.

The robots have their own language and can speak to one another. Without humans understanding what they're saying. Which is fine back here, where they're working for the good of mankind. But disastrous in LY500, when the Rebellion begins.

I turn away. And then I see it.

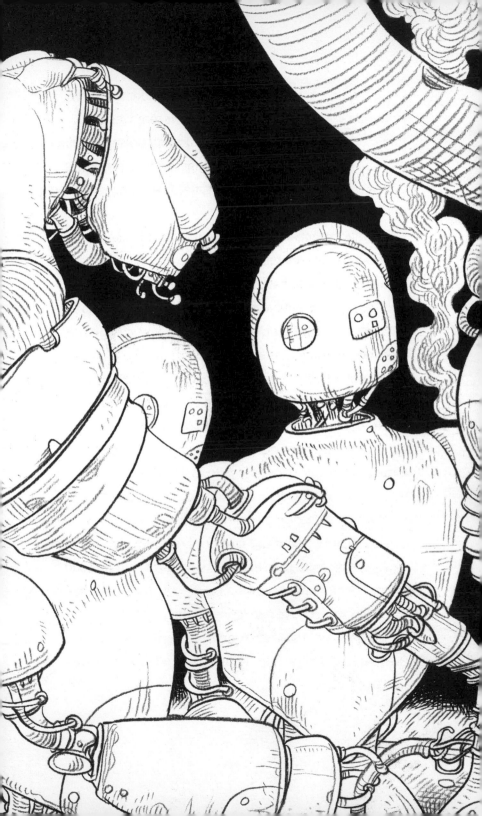

# 14

It's another robot, and it's heading straight towards me.

It looks busy. It's pushing a handcart that's filled with parts: a reflex engine and some lengths of T-cable. With its flashing eyes and fixed smile, it seems amiable enough. But hovering above its spherical head unit is a glowing green light.

It's the lazy 8 infinity symbol.

I turn away as slowly and smoothly as I can, then calmly cross the atrium, making sure I don't disturb the digital flow of the holographic scene around me. I walk around a table, step sideways to avoid an oncoming maintenance technician, then dip my head to pass beneath a low-hanging cable.

All the time, out of the corner of my eye, I can see the virus-scanner zoid roaming back and forth, probing the air for any disjoints.

I want to call out to Belle to get me out of here right now. But I don't dare. Even my voice, she has told me, is enough to create a ripple that the zoid would be able to detect.

74

If there's any trouble, Belle has instructed me to clear my conscious thoughts and head back to the entry point. And that's exactly what I'm aiming to do. The last

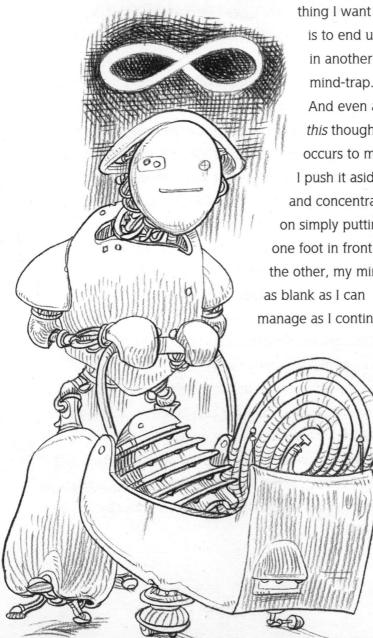

thing I want
is to end up
in another
mind-trap.
And even as
*this* thought
occurs to me,
I push it aside
and concentrate
on simply putting
one foot in front of
the other, my mind
as blank as I can
manage as I continue

making my way back to the elevator.

Halfway there, and a bunch of individuals burst into the room and head directly towards me. It's a relief team of workers, their shift over. Three men. Three robots. They're laughing and chatting together, almost like they're all friends.

I remain on my guard. One flapping holographic hand that passes through me, one jutting elbow or one misplaced foot, and the ripple in the digital flow will give me away.

I skirt round them, desperately hoping that nothing alerts the virus-scanner zoid to my presence.

Through the doorway at last, I head along the walkway as fast as I dare. I come to the elevator. It's all going well. So far. But I'm not safe yet. Other virus scanners are out and about. Six of them. They're circling around me like predators cruising through the ocean zone, their sensors on max alert.

The circles of dazzling light are back and I'm just about to step into them when . . .

Hot swarf! Where did *he* come from? I wonder, as a tech-engineer with an armful of motherboards appears out of nowhere and walks straight through me.

The air ripples. A high-pitched whine erupts.

And suddenly the virus scanners are onto me, all six of the Lazy 8 zoids homing in from all directions.

'*Belle!*' I scream.

For a horrible moment, I don't think she's heard me. The zoids surround me, their arms extended. Then, out of nowhere, the white-out comes, the blinding light obliterating the scene in front of me.

I'm back on the mind-ladder. And thank the Half-Lifes for that! Or rather, thank Belle . . .

'That was a close call,' I tell her.

'Too close,' Belle says darkly. 'They've locked on to the portal, York. The mind-ladder's no longer safe . . .'

I stare at her, not wanting to believe her words.

'Quick!' she tells me. 'You need to get out of here. Back through the portal and into another time and place. I'll track you. Now, York! *Now!*'

I'm in the havens again. Back before they were destroyed. And they look wonderful.

Back in my time, everywhere in the Outer Hull is so scuzzy. Centuries of dust and grime cling to every surface. Parasitic plants grow in the breaks in the floor plates and sprout from cracks in the pipes and tubes. And it's dangerous. Apart from killer zoids on the prowl, there are the countless weird mutant critters that have made it their home – winged predators, hordes of savage rodents and flesh-hungry creatures with claws and fangs – and are always hungry.

Here everything's new and clean and spotlessly maintained. And fascinating.

A woman flies overhead, riding a small bike-like hovercraft. It's sleek and silent, whisking its rider from A to B so much faster than if she was on foot – or even on one of the moving walkways that criss-cross the deck.

Where did they go, these hover-bikes? I wonder. Certainly there are none where I come from.

Just ahead of me, I see a man in a recliner. He's

wearing a holo-visor. There are other men and women around, on the balconies, on the walkways, all of them wearing the same visiglass devices. I don't understand how they work, but I notice how the people kind of stare into mid-air, talking . . .

Fact is, the whole place is packed with pieces of equipment that are technologically way ahead of anything we've got. A cyber-drone takes someone's temperature, while an environment unit cools the air with a soft mist. Mobile food-pods and aqua-jets offer refreshments. Holo-decks and tech-banks provide soothing images of oceans and sunsets from planet Earth.

The scanner on the wrist of the person before me reads *LY207*.

And not for the first time I find myself envying these humans from before the Rebellion. Where I come from, survival is a daily struggle. Back here, eight hundred years earlier, everything's been designed to ensure the well-being – physical and mental – of humans.

They had it so much easier than us, I realize. These humans back at the Launch Times.

I turn to see a bunch of people relaxing by a swimming pool. Some of them are in the water. Others are sitting in padded recliners, or lying on mats. Adults, children – and a squad of sleek silver robots that are taking care of all their needs.

'Greetwell, Marjorie,' one of the robots says as a middle-aged woman approaches, a towel tucked under her arm. 'If you'll allow me.'

'Greetwell, Boz,' she says.

The robot takes her towel, flaps it open and spreads it out on a reclining chair. Then, having plumped up the cushions, it helps the woman sit down.

'I have set the sun unit to thirty degrees Celsius. I hope it will be just the right temperature to help you recuperate after your hard day's work,' the robot, Boz, tells her. He hands her a sun visor and sprays an even film of UV-protector lotion over her face and body. 'And if you'll wait for just one moment . . .'

It shuffles off, to return seconds later with a silver tray balanced on its upraised hand. Its holo-face is smiling warmly.

'Vita-juice and energy nibbles,' it announces as it hands the tray over. 'I anticipated you would be ready for a little light refreshment, Marjorie.'

'Why, thank you, Boz,' says the woman, beaming with delight. 'That's most thoughtful of you.'

This robot is like a shinier, more streamlined version of the old personal helps. It's anticipating its owner's wishes, using its own initiative. Again, it seems harmless enough. But just like the robot communication I witnessed in the atrium, this development will prove to be deadly when the robots rebel.

All at once, the rings of dazzling light appear in front of me and I hear Belle's voice.

'I've found a data clue that might lead us to the first killer robot. To bad Mark . . .'

# 16

'The team of Mid Deck Zone 6 is pleased to announce an imminent new arrival,' a deck-com announces. 'Lin Tai the panda is about to give birth. For those interested, live visuals are available in vid-studios A and C and on com-tech lenses, code two-nine-six-four . . .'

I'm standing in one of the inter-level transporters, surrounded by people, about to descend from the Outer Hull to the Mid Deck – which is *really* weird, cos I'm in the Mid Deck already, aren't I? At least my body is. It's lying in a life-pod in an underground lab in Launch Year 1000. And Belle's in the pod beside me. But my consciousness is here, now, in the memory banks.

Which means we're in the same place at two different times . . .

Here, now, it's Launch Year 140, and I'm trying my best to take everything in as an extraordinary scene unfolds around me.

According to Belle, there are two main transporters on board, each of them a container-pod set into a broad shaft that connects the three levels of the Biosphere.

When the Rebellion took place, bio-engineers in the Mid Deck triggered a safety protocol that sealed them both off. But in Launch Year 140 they're working just the way they should be. They were designed to shift vast quantities of cargo from one part of the vessel to another, or when there's a need – like now – up to two hundred passengers.

That's why Belle opened the portal at this point. She says that, so long as I don't cause any digital ripples, it's harder for the virus scanners to track me in such a density of data. I hope she's right.

Once again, I'm struck by how happy and relaxed everyone looks. And with their high-def lenses and hyper-XT magnification offering them such a close-up view, I'm also surprised that they're so keen to witness the birth of this creature first-hand.

I suppose it's called human curiosity.

The container-pod I'm in is huge and square and clad with gleaming white polysynth panels. Soft electronic music is playing in the background. I guess it's meant to be soothing, but the kids all round me are so excited, nothing's going to calm them down.

'What *are* pandas?' one small boy is asking his mother.

'Oh, they're wonderful animals,' a woman in a dark blue tunic tells him. 'Big and fluffy, with black-and-white fur.' She smiles. 'And they eat nothing but bamboo.'

'Bamboo?'

'A kind of giant grass,' she tells him. 'It used to grow in the mountains of a place called China.'

'The panda was once the symbol for an Earth organization set up to prevent animal extinctions,' someone else chips in.

Up in the air, a holo-image of a creature with a white face and black eyes appears.

'Aaaah!' the kids sigh.

'Until they were all wiped out,' the man continues. 'First in the wild. Then in zoos . . .'

The kids' glee turns to a groan of disappointment.

'But there's been a special secret programme to bring them back, here in the Biosphere,' the mother tells her teary-eyed son. 'Using clone-tech and accelerated evolution. And it's working. It's into the third phase now. Five years ago they cloned a panda. A female. She's been in solitary confinement ever since. But now the bio-engineers have just announced that she's about to give birth – to a real live baby panda.'

And the kids all whoop and cheer. They're clearly overjoyed.

Me? I'm feeling a tad uneasy. Mention of accelerated evolution has brought back a whole load of bad memories. Back here in Launch Year 140, scientists had it under control. But after the robot rebellion, when everything got messed up, this advanced tech escaped from the labs in Zone 8 and turned the entire Mid Deck area into a vast nightmare filled with mutant critters and weird-looking humans.

A chaos zone . . .

The container-pod comes to a smooth halt. The doors glide open and, along with everyone else, I step out into the Mid Deck.

And my jaw drops.

Even with the improvements that the bird-woman,

Dextra, and her fellow scientists have started to make, the bio-zones of Launch Year 1000 are nothing like the amazing place spread out in front of me now. Buildings that were rusted and derelict stand tall and shiny; the broken walkways are up and running.

Someone in front of us pauses at an info-post and checks the directions on the holo-image glowing above it.

'Zone 6 is this way,' he announces, and, stepping onto one of the moving walkways, is whisked away.

Along with hundreds of others, I head the same way.

As we glide by the crew's living quarters and on through the Mid Deck, I stare in amazement at the bio-zones we pass. Every zone is kept separate from the one next to it. Each one is a magnificent reconstruction of a landscape I recognize from vid-screenings of life on Earth. They've got lookout towers, water troughs and feed-dispensers, and climate units that are suspended overhead on a network of cables. Every zone is enclosed by tall silver fences, with some of them electrified to keep the more dangerous species safely contained.

There are temperate woodlands that smell of sweet blossom and rotting vegetation. Sandy wastelands, the air oven-hot; then snowdrift plains, as cold as a deep freeze. Lush rainforest, dense jungle, swaying grassland and bubbling swamp. And the noise of the critters that live there! It's deafening! Whooping and roaring and howling and chittering and squawking and screeching . . .

'Look! Look!' the children shout, pointing out to one another the animals and birds they spot in the savannah zone.

My gaze comes to rest on animal after animal. And I'm amazed. These are not the mutations that I saw when I was last here. No, these are animals that evolved over millions of years on Earth, looking the way I know they should. Elephants, ostriches and zebras gathered round watering holes. Giraffes nibbling at acacia leaves. Families of warthogs. Prides of lions . . .

'A piece of Earth,' I mutter and, not for the first time, I'm impressed by just how clever the people back at the Launch Times were.

We arrive at Zone 6 and people start to step down from the walkway. They make their way to the front gates, where several uniformed men and women, along with a group of robots, are waiting.

'This way, this way,' they're saying as they lead the people into the zone.

And I go with them.

# 17

Walking in single file, we're led up a rocky mountain path that winds its way through a dense forest of spiky bamboo. We come to a circular visiglass enclosure. The walls are tinted so that we can see in, but the creature inside can't see out. One by one, all of the visitors take their seats on rows of urilium benches that surround the enclosure.

I stand at one end of a front-row bench. It would be so easy to walk *through* the visiglass wall into the enclosure, but that would create a telltale ripple in the data-stream and alert the virus scanners. So I remain outside.

A female panda is down on her haunches on a bed of chopped bamboo. She's rocking backwards and forwards, and emitting this soft grunting noise.

The children are oohing and aahing.

'It's so cute,' someone says.

Crouched down some way to the right of the panda is a man. He's wearing a white lab coat. And on the far side of him is a robot, which, apart from the glow of its eyes, is inactive.

I'm disappointed. Despite the data clue that Belle detected, this is not bad Mark. It's a similar model, but the head shape is different and the articulation of the arm units more sophisticated. Then I notice something else about it: something I don't like the look of.

Sluice it! The robot's armed.

It's the first one I've seen carrying weapons back here in the past. I can hardly believe it. After all, their protocol clearly states that their role is to serve.

But this one has the potential to injure, or even kill.

This, I realize, changes everything.

'Come on, Lin Tai,' the man is urging the panda gently. 'You can do it.'

And I hear the low murmur of encouraging voices all around me.

The panda continues to rock, growling softly as she does so. And as I look more closely, I see, nestling in her thick fur, a small, pink creature with closed eyes and stubby arms and legs. With a low grunt, the panda leans forward to lick it clean – but as she does so, she rolls onto the tiny infant.

And everything seems to happen at once . . .

The baby panda lets out a high-pitched squeal.

The keeper cries out and springs to his feet.

And the mother panda – startled and frightened and desperate to protect her newborn infant – goes for him, claws slashing and teeth bared.

The robot suddenly activates. It pivots round, raises an arm and fires its laser at the panda. A bolt of energy zaps her in the chest, and the creature drops to the ground like a stone.

A howl of misery erupts outside the enclosure. The children wail and burst into tears.

'It's all right,' the keeper is saying. He is crouching over the panda. 'She's just stunned. She'll be all right.'

And . . .' He checks the infant. 'And the baby's going to be just fine.'

He turns to the robot. 'You,' he says, angrily, 'leave the enclosure.'

'I believed you were in danger, sir,' it says, its voice calm and level. 'My role is to serve and protect you. That is my robotic protocol. I may not injure a human being –' its voice grows slightly louder and clearer – '*or through inaction cause a human being to come to harm.* I had no option but to fire—'

'Now!'

The robot turns obediently away. But I'm left shocked.

At some time in the past, someone must have decided to give the robots weapons. And what I have just seen in the panda enclosure proves that the robots were prepared to use them.

True, by protecting the human keeper from the animal attack, the robot *was* still keeping to the first law of its robotic protocol. But it has been given the potential to kill. And I know just how important – and deadly – that's going to be when the robots rebel.

My past is their future. If only there was something I could do to warn them. But of course, there isn't. And as the robot shuffles from the enclosure, the portal appears and I slip silently through it.

'That wasn't the robot we were looking for, Belle,' I tell her back on the mind-ladder. 'If we do find it—'

'*When* we find it,' Belle corrects me.

'*When* we find it,' I repeat, 'what then?'

'Then we track the record of it back through the memory banks until we find the exact moment when its primary protocol was altered.'

'The exact moment?' I ask.

'Yes, York,' she says. 'Only by seeing the exact moment the protocol was altered and the robot turned bad will we be able to identify the glitch. You see, York, it could be a billion different things – a malfunction in the manufacturing process, a speck of dust, a slight variation of temperature, a careless slip . . . A tiny glitch. Who knows what might have caused it? All I know is that something small caused a huge change.'

'You mean like that old story I heard from Earth that the flap of a butterfly's wing can cause a hurricane on the other side of the planet?' I ask.

She nods. 'Chaos theory,' she says. 'Exactly that, York.

But if we can spot what caused the glitch, we can take that information back to LY1000.'

'And save mankind?' I say.

Belle doesn't answer my question. Her face is taut with concentration.

'The virus scanners are still monitoring the portal to the mind-ladder,' she says. 'I've located a digital signature that might be evidence of a personal-help unit in Launch Year 38 that looks promising.'

'You mean Mark?' I say.

'Maybe,' says Belle. 'Prepare to let go, York.'

At first I have no idea where I am. Some kind of great hall. But then, as I make sense of the tall, curved objects that stand in a line on raised plinths along both side walls, my heart gives a leap.

These are mind-tombs.

There are hundreds of them. For the moment, they're empty and in blackness. But one day, I know, they will all bear the radiant faces of the Half-Lifes.

I hear the sound of voices singing a slow, sombre chant. It's coming from a corridor to my left.

Little by little, the chanting grows louder. It echoes round the vaulted ceiling, far above my head. Then, at the entrance, a figure appears. Dressed in a long black cape, the hood raised, he's at the head of a procession of men and women who are filing slowly and solemnly into the dimly lit hall.

I retreat into the shadows to watch.

I've never experienced anything like it before. The black robes that trail along the floor. The mournful singing. The slow steady *thump-thump* of heavy boots as, one after the other, the figures move across the hall. Hovering in the air between the tenth and the eleventh in line is a remote-control stretcher with two monitors – one glowing, one black – attached to its side. There's a motionless body lying on the stretcher.

I swallow uneasily. This is some kind of death ceremony. No sign of bad Mark though.

By the time the last person in the procession enters the hall, there are about fifty men and women gathered there. They move into position. One of the mind-tombs, I now see, has been removed from the line and is standing on its own at the centre of the gleaming floor. The hovering stretcher comes to a halt before it, with the dead man's head close to the curved casing at the front. The black-robed mourners form a circle around them.

Suddenly the chanting stops. The figure at the front of the procession steps forward and lowers his hood. He's a tall, thin man. And he looks distraught.

'We are gathered here for David Atherton,' the man says, his reedy voice cutting through the silence. 'He was a dependable colleague and a wonderful friend.'

Atherton? I know who that is! I met him as a Half-Life on the viewing deck of the Outer Hull.

I must be in Year 38. Thirty-eight years after the Biosphere was launched from Earth. That's the year he told me he'd died.

'People credit me, Samuel Marston, mission commander,' the man continues, 'with the creation of this great space mission of ours. The Father of the Biosphere, they call me. And it is true – it was my dream to leave the dying Earth with our precious cargo, examples of all that was good about our planet, and journey to a new world for humankind to colonize.'

He pauses and I see his eyes mist over.

'A dream . . . And that is what it would have remained, had it not been for David Atherton.'

The circle of figures mutter their agreement, and I see their heads nod up and down.

'For it was David Atherton who made it all possible,' Marston goes on. 'He coordinated the building of our vessel. He organized the launch. And since the Biosphere departed the Earth, it was he, with responsibility for two thousand crew and twenty thousand robots, who made our mission a success. So far. Now we must learn to cope without him. Except . . .'

Marston raises a hand and gestures towards the mind-tomb. It begins to glow, and loops of red light flow up and down the curved outer casing. At the same time, bands of green light encircle the hovering stretcher and ripple along the motionless body upon it.

'Sadly David Atherton's body is on the point of giving out. But his mind,' he goes on, his outstretched fingers flicking from the first monitor to the second, where a series of jagged lines are moving across the screen, 'is as sharp as it ever was. And it is his mind – his wisdom, his knowledge, his memories – that will live on in this, the first mind-tomb to be activated, so that in death David Atherton might guide us the way he did when he was alive. Forever.'

Once again, a murmur of approval ripples round the hall.

As I continue to watch, something happens. The coloured lines begin to fuse. The red of the mind-tomb and the green of the body come together to form a great swirling dome that encloses them both and glows an intense golden yellow. Brighter and brighter it shines, and as it does so, the air fills with a piercing whine – before abruptly cutting out.

The afterglow fades, and I see that the mind-tomb now has a face glowing from within it. The jowly, smiley face of an old man with short greying hair and clear blue eyes.

Atherton's face.

The face nods at Marston, then at the gathering of people around him. 'Greetwell,' it – he – says softly.

And, as one, everyone in the hall responds. 'Greetwell.'

With the ceremony over, the crowd of people starts to file out. Soon the hall is empty. Only Marston remains.

The man is grieving, the expression on his face grim. He stoops down over the hovering stretcher and pulls the shroud back to reveal his dead friend. He wipes away a tear, then looks up at the Half-Life.

'I will come and talk with you often, David, old friend,' he says.

And Atherton smiles, his holographic face glowing from within the mind-tomb. 'I hope that it will be a long time before you join me here,' he says. 'But when you do, it will be a price worth paying in order to continue our work. Guiding the crew, advising them, counselling them . . .'

Marston gives a small nod. 'It will,' he agrees.

But as he turns away I see a look pass across the mission commander's face – a look of barely concealed horror.

He strides across the hall to the entrance. And there, standing in the doorway, is a personal-help unit. I gasp. Has Belle done it?

Is this Mark, the robot that went bad? It certainly looks like him. The same model. And though it's difficult to see clearly in the dim light, I think I can see a scratch down the left side of its head.

'Follow me,' Marston tells the dumpy robot as he leaves, and the two of them head together down a long shadowy corridor.

I'm about to follow them, when the floor gives a sudden lurch and everything goes black . . .

# 20

With a violent jolt, I gulp at the air and sit up. I open my eyes.

Belle's looking down at me. She's holding me tightly by the arm. I'm lying in the pod in the Mid Deck. Behind her is the chief scientist of the Mid Deck bio-zones, Dextra. I've got to know her well during my time here. She is a genetically modified human with feathered wings, which I see quivering at her shoulders as she looks back at me.

'Oh, York,' she says, as she reaches forward and wipes the sweat from my brow. 'We lost all power to the life-pods for a moment. And we thought we'd lost you too.'

My head's swimming and my legs tingle with pins and needles.

As Dextra carefully disconnects the brain monitors and sustenance feeds, I feel the suckers tugging at the skin on my forehead and temples, then hear a soft, squelchy hiss as air gets in and, one after the other, they come free. There's a sharp pain in

my arms as the tubes are pulled from my veins.

'Are you all right, York?' the bird-woman asks.

Her voice seems louder than usual. More . . . I don't know. I can hear every sound she's making so clearly. The shifting vowel sounds as her mouth changes shape.

And the way she looks!

It's like I'm staring at her through a magnifying glass. I can see every pore on her skin, every hair on her head, every feather in her wings. I've never seen everything so clearly before.

I look round me. The lab seems to be throbbing with dazzling colour. And the computer banks. *And* the people working at them. The tables, the tools, the cabinets, the racks, the overhead lamps: gaudy and crystal clear, the whole lot. I know it sounds crazy, but it's like I'm seeing everything in three dimensions for the very first time.

'Are you all right?' Dextra says again. She sounds concerned.

'I'm fine,' I tell her, and, as if to prove it, I climb out of the pod.

But too quickly. I feel dizzy and my legs go weak. I reach out and grip the side of the pod to steady myself, and close my eyes, waiting for the spinning to stop.

'How long were we down there?' I hear Belle asking Dextra, and to me her voice echoes strangely.

'Eight days,' comes the reply.

Eight days! I can hardly believe it.

Belle turns to me. 'The transportation's taken a lot out of you,' she says gently. 'I created the mind-ladder to help you navigate safely. But you're human. And the human brain is fragile.' Her voice drops to a low whisper. 'I hope no damage has been caused—'

'We'll run some tests,' Dextra breaks in, and she takes my arm.

And hot swarf! The feel of *that*! It's incredible, like every nerve ending on my skin is raw.

I open my eyes again. Dextra and Belle are both looking at me. My head's still swimming, but my legs are feeling a bit more sturdy now.

'What's going on?' I ask.

'It's what happens when you've spent any time in the pod,' says Dextra. 'While you were inside it, everything you experienced was in your mind. All holographic images from the memory banks. Now it's for real – and all the more vivid for that.'

'It's like my senses are on overload,' I tell her.

'Which means that this should taste extra delicious,' comes a voice, and I turn to see my friend Cronos, another scientist with modified wings, walking towards me. He has a tray of food and drink in his hands. He frowns. 'You are hungry, I take it?'

'*So* hungry!' I say.

He smiles. 'Then follow me.'

We head through the door into the next room. It's small, with a low ceiling and shuttered windows. Cronos sets the plates and mugs down on a table, and I pull up a seat opposite him. Then, stomach rumbling and mouth watering, I tuck in.

And Cronos is right. The juicy green stuff, the meaty brown stuff, the creamy yellow stuff . . . I don't know what it is, but it's all fantastic. Food has never tasted so good.

Belle and Dextra join us at the table just as I'm washing down my last bite with a mouthful of dark spicy bev.

'The life-pods have been downloading everything you experienced in the memory banks,' Dextra says. 'But they cut out just at the end of the mind-tomb ceremony . . .'

'I saw him . . . it! The bad robot, Mark. I'm sure I did,' I tell them all excitedly. 'I was about to follow it when everything went black.'

Cronos shakes his head. 'I'm sorry about that,' he says. 'We've been experiencing power cuts and we suspect the zoids of the Outer Hull are responsible.'

'The life-pods have been damaged,' Dextra adds. 'It'll take some time to repair them. I'll get the Sanctuary droids onto it straight away.'

'In the meantime,' says Cronos, 'there are some people I'd like you to meet. York, Belle, come with me.'

As we walk down a long corridor towards the

entrance, I look out of the visiglass windows on both sides. It's amazing. So much has been achieved in the eight days since I was last here.

Everywhere I look, modified humans and Sanctuary-dwellers are working together to repair and maintain the bio-zones. In the savannah region, the perimeter fences are being repaired. Beyond that, I see the polar region, where white-furred animals are prowling ice floes. Squawks and howls echo from the rainforest region. And when I look up I see the dome of the Sanctuary gleaming far off in the distance.

Working alongside these humans are droids. Lots of them. Shiny and sleek, just like the robots from before the Rebellion. Not surprising really, because when the robot rebellion started, the three levels of the Biosphere were sealed off by humans. These Mid Deck robots and droids were never contaminated by the glitch – or whatever it was that turned the others against humans.

'We have re-activated the inter-level transportation unit,' Cronos says. 'I personally led a group of us to make contact with the Outer Hull-dwellers. We managed to bring a number of them back to the safety of the Mid Deck. But the zoids detected us.' He sighs. 'We had a narrow escape—'

At that moment, the quiet is shattered by a deafening siren.

'Perhaps I spoke too soon,' Cronos breathes.

Suddenly, through the windows, it looks like the whole place has gone crazy.

Great clouds of dust are flying up inside the fenced-in zone just ahead, as herds of horned creatures stampede. They're hurtling over the dried-out grassland, bellowing and snorting, then crashing into the perimeter fence, desperate to escape something I can't even see. A striped creature with flapping ears and a long tail seizes her cub in her mouth and dashes off. Small brown furry critters scrabble frantically at the sand before disappearing into the holes they've dug.

And the people. Sanctuary-dwellers. Modified humans. They're acting as terrified as the critters, all racing off in the same direction, glancing back over their shoulders. They're being helped by the droids. The tiny lens-head droids are guiding them as best they can, while tripod droids are carrying the injured to the safety of the Sanctuary dome.

But why? What is happening?

Some of the people, I notice, are already wearing safe-suits. Some have dark visiglass visors on; others, padded ear-protectors. Others are putting on oxygen masks as they run, or are helping others to do so, pulling them over their faces.

There's something wrong out there. It's affecting both critters and humans. And everyone is trying their best to keep themselves safe from whatever it is . . .

A stocky gill-man lumbers past close to the window I'm crouched behind. In his hands is an oxygen mask that he's struggling to unfasten so he can put it on. All at once though, he trips, stumbles, falls and the mask bounces off across the hard earth. He scrambles towards it.

Then something else happens. Something bad. Face twisted up with pain, he clutches at his head. His eyes roll back and he slumps down heavily to the ground, his body rigid.

He does not move.

A wing-man flying overhead swoops down. He's wearing a helmet complete with goggles, ear-protectors and a breathing tube. Landing next to the gill-man, he tries to shift him. But the body is too heavy and, clearly frightened, the wing-man flies off again empty-handed.

'What do you think's going on, Belle?' I ask.

But she doesn't answer me.

I turn to see her staring intently at one particular person. A girl, one hand fluttering at the face mask she's wearing, making sure it's securely in place. She's running towards us at the head of a group of some ten or twelve people.

They're not dressed like Sanctuary-dwellers. Instead they're wearing hooded flakcoats, with grenbolts at their belts and backcans on their shoulders. They reach the entrance, the door slides open and they come tumbling in. The door closes behind them.

The girl reaches up, unclips the mask, raises her tinted visor and lowers her hood. Long blonde hair tumbles down over her shoulders and face, and she pushes it back to reveal a pair of large blue eyes.

My heart misses a beat.

'York!' she exclaims.

'Lina!'

# 22

The two of us fall into each other's arms. It's been such a long time since we last saw each other.

Lina is one of my oldest friends. We grew up together at the Inpost. I haven't seen her since Belle and I left the Outer Hull and set off for the Mid Deck.

We hug tightly, and it feels good. At first. But Lina clings on for too long and I start to feel awkward. And when I try to pull away, she just hugs me all the tighter.

'You're . . . crushing . . . me . . .' I grunt, putting on a kind of being-crushed voice.

And still she doesn't let go. It's only when someone else comes across to us, and I hear, 'Lina, put him down!' that she finally releases her grip.

'Dek!' I exclaim. 'You're here too!'

Dek is my *best* friend! He's looking good. Beefier than before and with a sharp new haircut. And as for his false arm, he's got this new one that looks much better than the one Bronx made him. With the synth-skin and fingernails, it looks just like the real thing.

'These are a couple of the scavengers we encountered

on our mission to the Outer Hull, York,' Cronos says, turning away from the window. 'I thought you'd be pleased to see them . . .'

'Oh, York,' Lina cries out, suddenly grabbing hold of my hand, 'you don't know what it's like up there. Humans are either being killed or turned into the zoids' slaves. And we can't hold out much longer. Bronx needs you. We *all* need you.'

'The zoids have gone through several upgrades since you left,' Dek says, and grimaces. 'And each time they do, they make themselves bigger, more powerful. They've become pretty much invincible . . .'

I release myself from Lina's grip and turn to him.

'No zoid's invincible,' I tell him. 'We're cleverer than them. Always were, always will be. Hot swarf! You and me, Dek, we're scavengers. The zoid doesn't exist that we can't zilch.'

'Not any more,' Lina says desperately. She looks close to tears. 'All those experiments they did on us humans – uploading our minds into their computer banks – they've learned things about us.' She shakes her head. 'Half the time they don't even use weapons any more. All they need to do is make it too hot or too cold, or cut off the oxygen supply . . .'

'Or release some kind of knock-out gas,' says Cronos darkly, casting an eye outside. 'If that's what they've done.'

'I don't think there's anything wrong with the air,' says Dek. 'Any toxic gases would have shown up on our detectors. And yet—'

'It's like there was something inside my head,' Lina interrupts. 'I couldn't *hear* anything.' She pauses. 'But I could *feel* it.'

Dek's nodding. 'Kind of scrambling my brain.'

Just then Dextra comes running in, her face pale.

'There's been some kind of sonic attack!' she says. 'Sound waves used as a weapon. The upper frequencies we recorded are off the scale.'

'Enough to knock a person out?' asks Cronos.

'Enough to kill a person if it goes on long enough,' says Dextra, her wings shuddering. 'Thankfully it's stopped now.'

'Maybe it was just an experiment,' says Cronos. 'To see what would happen.' He shakes his head grimly. 'The zoids are learning more and more about us all the time, and—'

'Which is why you're wanted back in the Outer Hull, York,' Lina interrupts. 'Now. The humans up there are in such danger, and you could help them. The survivors. According to Bronx, you're the best scavenger we've got.'

'Bronx?' I say.

Lina's face flushes. She looks down. 'Now he's a Half-Life,' she says, 'I get to talk to him all the time.'

'And he mentioned me?' I say.

'Yes, yes, y . . . yes, he did,' she says. Her voice sounds shallow and breathless. 'He's concerned about you, York,' she adds, and flashes me a smile which disappears behind her hand as she scratches her nose. 'He says you're to come back to the Outer Hull straight away—'

'You can't, York,' Belle breaks in. Her voice is calm. 'We have a mission to complete.'

'*Mission?*' Lina explodes. She turns her anger on me. 'You're going to let her tell you what to do? This . . . this *machine*! We need you, York. The

Outer Hull needs you. Bronx needs you . . .'

'You're lying,' Belle says.

'What did you say?' Lina hisses furiously.

'You are lying to York,' Belle says evenly.

Lina is struck dumb. Her cheeks go red and blotchy and her mouth opens and closes, but no words come out.

'Your body language gave you away,' Belle continues. 'The colour of your face. The tightness in your chest. The exaggerated movements of your head. The way you covered up your mouth with your hand . . .'

Lina is weeping silently now, tears running down her cheeks.

'Hush, Belle,' I tell her, then take Lina by her hands.

'Oh, York,' Lina says tearfully, and I can see that she knows she's been caught out. 'I'm sorry. But I've been so worried about you. Down here, doing who knows what. I couldn't bear it if you got hurt. I just want you back safely.' She flashes a hurt and angry look at Belle. 'Where you belong.'

'It's all right,' I say softly. I squeeze her hands, smile. 'I understand. So *does* Bronx have a message for me?' I ask her.

Lina nods jerkily. 'He . . . he said . . .' She hangs her head. 'Tell him I'll see him in the Halls of Eternity.'

# 23

The warning siren is still wailing outside when a lens-
head droid flies along the corridor towards us. It comes
to a halt in mid-air and hovers at Cronos's shoulder.

'Sensors detect Inter-Level Transporter 2 activated,' its
mechanical voice announces. 'Arrival imminent.'

Tight-lipped, Cronos nods. 'Get all the fighting men and
women to meet at the muster points,' he orders. 'Ensure
that ammunition packs are full and energy-pods charged.'

With a buzz, the lens-head turns in the air and speeds
off to spread the word.

Cronos turns to us. 'I was afraid of this,' he says. 'The
zoids have taken over the Outer Hull. Now they want
to do the same in the Mid Deck. And we can't let that
happen. We need to get to the transporters and seal
them off.' His eyes darken. 'Are you with me?'

'We're with you,' we say as one.

Cronos turns and strides down the corridor towards
the entrance, and the rest of us go too.

There are twelve in our small group. Me and Belle,
Lina and Dek, as well as a whole bunch of other

scavengers that Cronos rescued from the Outer Hull. One of them I recognize. His name is Tex, and he's about my age. The pair of us first met back at the Fulcrum. It would be good to catch up, but there's no time right now.

'Stick together,' Cronos tells us as he steps through the doorway.

Outside, the sonic attack seems to be over. Certainly nothing is registering on our audio monitors. But we keep ear-protectors at the ready, just in case. And, following Cronos, we head towards Transporter 2 as fast as we can.

Some of the larger creatures in the zones are beginning to stir, though the humans who were subjected to the high-frequency sound waves for too long are still out cold. Mid Deck droids are moving among them, I notice, doing their best to tend to their needs.

Up in the ceiling the arc-lights are fading. Night's coming on.

After a while, Cronos abruptly turns off the path we're taking and strides away into the trees of the rainforest zone. The air smells rank. The leaves drip with moisture. There's birdcry and crittercall.

The lens-head has done its work. Armed men and women have gathered. Lots of them. And as we head through the forest, more join our group. Modified humans for the most part – wing-men, fur-men, lizard-men and a solitary gill-man – plus three hefty-looking

former guards from the Sanctuary.

'Greetwell,' Cronos says to each of them in turn. 'Keep close, all of you.'

At the far side of the rainforest we pass a square sump pool – where more gill-men are climbing up out of the black water – and emerge from the trees into a sort of paved clearing. Ahead of us is a broad urilium shaft that stretches from floor to ceiling. Set into it at ground level are huge double doors. There are vines and creepers clinging to the metallic outer casing now, but I recognize the place at once. I saw it when I was down in the memory banks.

This is the entrance to one of the inter-level transporters. A large peeling number 2 painted on the doors confirms that we've come to the right one.

Above the doors is a light panel. And it's on, glowing red. From somewhere deep inside the transporter, I hear the throbbing hum of the container-pod approaching. Then the red light starts to flash . . .

'Take cover,' Cronos commands.

Too late to seal the transporter from any intruders now, we retreat into the undergrowth. Belle and I duck down behind an abandoned feed-trough and hide ourselves as best we can. I switch on my coolant-suit to mask my heat-sig.

The hum of the approaching container-pod grows louder.

I peer out through the bars of the rusting trough. A small herd of deer-like critters with corkscrew horns have appeared from the forest and are milling about. A troop of monkeys with long scaly tails are leaping about the surrounding trees, noisily searching for food. And there are two of the work droids from the zones walking past, unaware that anything is wrong . . .

Abruptly the hum cuts out. The light turns green.

I hold my breath. There's a soft clunk, followed by a low hiss as the huge doors slide apart and light streams out from inside the container-pod.

'It looks empty,' I whisper to Belle.

But she puts a finger to her lips and shakes her head.

All around me, from various points in the tangle of undergrowth, I hear the others prime their weapons. The *click-click* of grenbolts ratcheting into position. The whining hum of stunners as they power up for action. I pull my pulser from my belt and aim it at the opening. Beside me, Belle draws her cutter . . .

I wait, silent, still, holding my breath.

Dek and Lina both mentioned the latest zoid upgrades, and I wonder what monstrosities we're about to be confronted by. Then, inside the container-pod, I see movement, and silhouetted against the bright white light something lurches stiffly forward.

And I cannot believe my eyes . . .

# 24

It's a human. A man.

He's thin and dead-eyed. Drool hangs in glistening strands from the corners of his mouth. I stare at him in horror as he shuffles out from the container-pod and into the overgrown clearing.

I've seen someone just like him before, I remember. Down in the memory banks.

He's not alone. Behind him is a line of other humans. Men and women, each one as zombie-like as the man they are following. Their clothes are little more than rags; tattered flakcoats, patched breeches, scuffed boots. In contrast, the metal bands around their necks look new. Made of shiny urilium, they're studded with a row of small white lights that switch on and off in a flickering sequence.

'What are they, Belle?' I breathe.

'Control-collars,' Belle whispers back. 'So far as I can make out with my sensors, the zoids are using them to make the humans carry out their commands.'

Humans, drained of their own consciousness, forced

to obey the zoids. The thought of it horrifies me. I watch their awkward movements as, legs stiff and eyes unblinking, they stumble forward. If they're doing the zoids' bidding, they could be dangerous – though so far as I can see, they're not armed.

'Hold your fire,' I hear Cronos call. 'But remain hidden.'

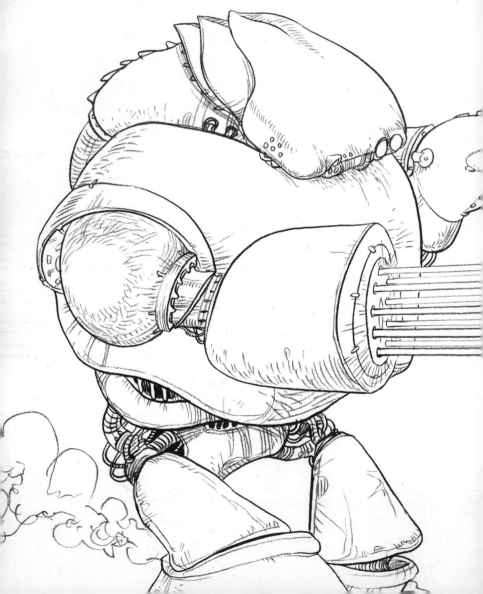

We do as we're told. Watching. Waiting.

The place is in night-mode now. All the arc-lights are off except for one, which shines down brightly like a full moon. The deer-like critters are skittering about uneasily. The monkeys' chatter and whoop has fallen silent.

The zombie-like humans jerk to a halt.

All at once the air explodes with the harsh stutter of automatic gunfire and the orange dazzle of exploding tracer bullets. From somewhere to my left I hear a muffled cry, followed by a thud as someone hits the

ground. Maybe the humans are armed after all. Maybe the urilium control-collars are forcing them to attack.

But when the second burst of bullets and laser fire

explodes, I realize that isn't what's happening. The weapons are not being fired by the humans, but by something behind them – which is when I notice the light glinting on polished metal further back inside the container-pod.

Zoids. Tons of them. And they're using their zombie prisoners as a human shield.

Cronos's commands fill the air.

'Scavengers, hold back!' he's shouting. 'Be ready for when the zoids break through.' He pauses. Then, '*Attack!*' he roars.

From several points at the edge of the forest, Mid-Deckers emerge. Weapons drawn, the wing-men take to the air, fly over the top of the line of lurching humans and fire down on the zoids behind. Lizard-men join them, kicking off with their powerful legs, and leaping over the heads of the humans before opening fire. Fur-men and gill-men barrel forward, trusting that their thick skin will be enough to repel the zoids' tracer-fire. Though as I watch, first one, then a second, brave Mid-Decker is brought down.

Not that the zoids are getting it all their own way. Swooping and diving, the wing-men are taking them out. So are the lizard-men. Then, from somewhere to my right I hear the telltale click of a frack-grenade pin being pulled, and I look round to see the muscular arm of a fur-man tossing the primed weapon over the heads of the zombie-like humans and inside the container-pod.

With a loud bang and a blinding flash, the grenade explodes and the air is filled with white-hot scraps of metal as a zoid is blown up.

The Mid-Deckers are trying their best not to harm any of the humans as they launch attack after attack on the zoids. But casualties are inevitable. As the human shield continues to lurch awkwardly forward, I see a woman struck by a chunk of flying debris. Then a man, lasered in the back by a zoid, stumbles and falls. The pair of them slam down to the ground, where they remain, their bodies twitching as the control-collars compel them to keep advancing.

'We need to get them out of there,' I tell Belle, as familiar-looking killer zoids start gliding through the gaps in the human shield, firing wildly.

Belle nods, but before either of us can act, the two droids I saw earlier head towards them and start tending to the injured humans. They seem oblivious to the fact that we're in the middle of a pitched battle.

But then one of the killer zoids stops firing. It turns to the droids and I see it reach out with its extendable arms and seize the pair of them in its grasp. A zigzag bolt of electro-static passes between them, and when it switches off, the droids' yellow eyes show that they have turned as bad as all the rest.

Before they can move, two shots ring out. Laser fire zaps the droids in their chests, zilching them, and they clatter to the ground.

'Get all remaining droids back to the Sanctuary to avoid further contamination,' I hear Cronos bellow.

The next moment he's beside me. There's a lens-head droid buzzing at his shoulder.

'York,' he says. 'Just the person I wanted to see.'

'Is it time to return fire?' I say. 'We'll take good care not to hit any more of the people in the human shield, and . . .'

But Cronos is shaking his head. 'I've just received fresh information,' he tells me urgently. 'This assault here is nothing but a diversion. The main attack is about to take place at Inter-Level Transporter number one.'

'Number one,' I repeat numbly.

'It's on the far side of the ocean zone,' Belle tells me.

Cronos nods. 'I want you two, together with your band of scavengers, to be there waiting for them when they arrive,' he says. 'Then deal with them.' He nods back to the killer zoids. 'We'll hold this lot off as best we can. Go,' he says urgently. 'Go now. Before it's too late.'

It doesn't feel right leaving the others while the battle is still raging. But if Cronos's info is correct, there's no choice.

I stick two fingers in my mouth and whistle loudly – three short, sharp bursts. It's something Bronx taught me, years back. The scavengers gather for instructions. And then we're off, hightailing it to Transporter 1.

The most direct route there is through the polar zone. But with the refrigerator units up and running once more, and the temp an even minus twelve, the place is just too cold. Instead, Belle leads us round the perimeter fence. And then, when we come to the thick visiglass walls of the vast ocean-zone tank, she takes us down a staircase that leads underneath it.

'A short cut,' she explains. 'We'll make up the time we've lost.'

We race down the stairs and along the corridor, passing droids that are busy repairing the lighting system. The floor is paved with touch-sensitive light panels that come on, one after the other, as we tread on them. And Belle's right. We should make up the time – and definitely would do, if it wasn't for my fellow scavengers.

Born and raised in the Outer Hull, they've never seen anything like the display of weird sea critters through the visiglass ceiling above our heads. Scarcely able to believe their eyes, they keep stopping for a closer look. At the darting shoals of tiny silver fish. At the prowling sharks and ink-squirting squid. At the eels and sea horses, anemones and crabs, and the ordered battalions of stripy cuttlefish . . .

Fact is, *everything* seems to fascinate them.

'Is that an octopus?' I hear Tex ask Lina, and turn to see that they've fallen back yet again.

'We don't have time for this,' I shout at them. 'Keep up.'

Finally we all make it to the other side. Belle climbs the staircase two steps at a time, and we race after her. We emerge in the open air next to a box-shaped power unit and an info post.

*Zone 7 : Mediterranean.*

And to the right of that is Inter-Level Transporter 1.

The light panel above the huge double doors is still red – but I can hear the deep hum of the approaching container-pod from inside the shaft. The zoids will be here at any moment. So far I've only seen familiar types of killer zoids. But if this is the main attack, I'm guessing they'll have saved the most-dangerous zoids for now.

'You said they'd upgraded,' I say to Lina and Dek. 'What can we expect?'

'All sorts,' says Lina.

'Your worst nightmare,' Dek adds.

We should prepare for their arrival, I realize. And if they're as bad as Dek and Lina are saying, then we're going to need more than gunkballs and cutters.

Question is, what?

Then I remember something I witnessed in the memory banks. How Dirk Miller and the group of scientists zilched that zoid, way back when the Rebellion started . . .

I hurry across to the power unit and pull the front cover off. Inside is a tangled mess of wires and cables. I locate the induction-flux hub and switch the energy off. Throughout the Mediterranean zone, lights go off, pumped water stops flowing and the buzzing air falls silent.

'These need to be spread out in front of the transporter doors,' I say, as I pull out the bundle of black cables and multicoloured wires from the power unit, unravel them and start to feed them out to my fellow scavengers.

Working together, Lina, Dek, Tex and the others lay them out. Soon, the wires are spread in a large rectangle in front of the doors and every centimetre of the ground is covered in a criss-cross grid.

'It looks like some kind of doormat,' Dek comments.

'A welcome mat,' I say, drawing my cutter. 'We're going to give them a welcome they won't ever forget.'

Dropping to my knees, I start stripping the safety casing away, exposing the metal wires inside. The others join in. The colourful mat turns to silver.

Above the double doors of the transporter, the light panel starts flashing red.

'Pull back!' I yell. 'Take cover!'

As the others retreat, I race to the power unit and crouch down. A single cable connects all the wires we've laid out to the induction-flux hub. I only hope it holds.

The light turns green.

I crouch down. Look round. I can't see Belle, and it occurs to me that I haven't seen her since we first arrived at the transporter. I'd call out for her, but it's too late now. The doors are sliding open . . .

# 26

Just like before, light comes pouring out of the transporter unit. But this time, instead of zombie-like humans appearing at the entrance, it's zoids. Upgrades. Monstrous upgrades, standing in a long line . . .

'Hot swarf,' I murmur.

One has six long pneumatic legs that hiss as they flex. Mounted on them is a huge disc-shaped body, with lights and antennae dotted over the shiny urilium surface, and three retractable arms that are armed with lasers and rocket launchers.

The next zoid is different. It's at least twice as tall as the first, and supported on what look like hundreds of stubby metal digits. It has a broad angular midsection, with four flexible arms sticking out on all sides. Each arm is round and jointed and tipped with different devices: pincers, probes and the gleaming barrels of heavy laser weaponry.

The third is different again. Made up of two parts, it looks like some kind of articulated vehicle. The front half has piston-like legs; the back half, hinged units that look

as if they're designed to jump . . .

And so it goes on. There are twelve, so far as I can make out. Each zoid is different from the one next to it, unique in design and purpose. The only thing they all have in common is that, unlike old-style robots, none of these upgrades looks anything like a human being. These are machines, made by machines, for machines.

Invincible, Dek said they were, and now I can see why.

Just then there's a whirring, buzzing, droning noise. It's coming from the line of zoids, and I see their weapons flash and vibrate as they power up. Then there are more noises. Bleeps and trills, along with other sounds so deep I can barely hear them – though I can *feel* them. One zoid jerks into motion. Another shuffles forward, the lights on its outer casing pulsing. A third, further along the line, raises an arm.

They're communicating with one another, I realize. Assessing the situation here in the Mid Deck. Making plans . . .

Suddenly all the zoid lights start to flash in unison. The noises cease. The zoids march forward.

My shaking hand hovers above the induction-flux hub. Split-second timing is crucial if this is going to work. I have to keep my nerve.

I watch the first zoid step out of the container-pod and down onto the silvery blanket of exposed wires. Then the second. Then the third. I wait until the first zoid is in the middle of the booby trap we've laid – then slam my hand down hard on the flux-hub unit.

The energy comes back on and . . .

There's a colossal *BOOM!* and a blinding flash of blue-white light as the power shorts and arcs. The six long pneumatic legs of the zoid at the front of the line kick out wildly, sparks streaming from the articulated joints. The curved body rocks and sways, and the weapons start to fire at random, shooting lasers and frack-rockets.

I stand stock-still, mesmerized, as they scythe down branches and explode in the air.

There's loud crackling and hissing, and a dazzling jagged halo of light suddenly surrounds the zoid. Its light units flash, then explode. Steaming gunk-juice spurts from cracks that appear in its white-hot outer casing. It swivels, jerks. It lurches backwards, then forwards, then backwards again, attempting to maintain balance. Then, giving up the struggle, the whole lot keels backwards . . .

And slams into the second zoid.

Which topples back against the third . . .

They tumble like dominoes – one after the other – completing the circuit and causing the electro-pulse to course through their systems. The booby trap is working. Motherboards short out. Weapons explode. Soon all twelve zoids have been zilched.

Of course, I tell myself, there are bound to be masses more deadly upgrade zoids back in the Outer Hull. We humans might still not win the war. But this is one battle that we *have* won, and I feel proud to have been a part of it . . .

But I've spoken too soon. My stomach churns as I stare into the container-pod.

'Uh-oh,' I groan.

The thirteenth killer zoid is bigger and meaner-looking than all the rest. While the others lie in a long unbroken chain where they've fallen, their smoking bodies inactive, this thirteenth zoid glides silently forward.

It's immense, standing at least five metres tall. A small domed head unit with a single light set into the front is mounted on a broad barrel-shaped torso. It's got arms, six of them. And they're fitted with a fearsome array of weapons. Stack lasers. Alpha-ray diffusers. Taser-spikes. UV missiles. Frack-grenade repeater units . . .

I've never seen a zoid so well armed.

The one thing it doesn't have is legs. Instead three pipes are fixed to the bottom of the torso unit, each one shooting down a  vertical jet of hot air that allows it to hover *above* the ground – unaffected by the electro-pulse.

'Scavengers at the ready!' I shout as the zoid glides out of the container-pod.

It moves slowly over the metal floor of the container pod and the sparking blanket of wires. Pausing for a moment above the burned-out zoids, it inspects the damage. Its headpiece swivels. Bleeps. Then it moves on, towards the trees.

I wonder where my fellow scavengers have got to. In this kind of situation, we have two choices. One, to remain hidden. Two, to attack. But with a zoid this well tooled-up, that would be desperately risky . . .

The air seems to throb with tension.

Suddenly I catch a flash of movement. And I might have known. It's Belle. She's leaping down from the top of one of the pine trees and lands on the zoid's back. Then, legs wrapped tightly round its upper section, she clamps one hand over the light on its head and raises her other arm high in the air. The cutter she's holding glints in the single arc-light.

The next moment, with unbelievable speed and immense power, she brings her arm down. The blade of the cutter slams down into the narrow gap between the zoid's domed head unit and its barrel-shaped torso. Thick grey-green zoid-juice spurts back into her face . . .

And she loses her grip.

The zoid lurches from side to side, the hover-jets hissing intermittently as one, then the other, shuts off and on. It's malfunctioning. But it hasn't given up. And as I watch, the arm with the taser-spike bends upwards.

The weapon hums as it charges up to max power. It

begins to glow. The tip of the spike sparks as it closes in on Belle's back . . .

'Stop!' a voice cries out, and I turn to see someone racing out of the trees.

'Lina!' I shout.

Then Dek and Tex appear behind her. It all happens so fast. Before I can so much as move, the zoid swivels around, buzzing, bleeping, scans Dek and Tex, then gets Lina in its sights.

And fires . . .

But not before Lina has thrown herself to the ground and rolled over. As I watch, she pulls herself up to a low crouch, aims her pulser and fires back. The zoid lurches to one side. Lina fires again. And again. And Belle, wiping the gunk from her eyes, scrambles up the zoid's massive shoulder unit and slams down with the cutter a second time.

This time, the blade penetrates the zoid's central control-mode. The lights go out and, with one last sputter, the hover-jets shut off. Belle jumps free as it topples to one side. The next moment, the zoid hits the ground with a loud crash.

Belle picks herself up. She's undamaged. She looks around and, seeing Lina still lying on the floor, her pulser drawn, she crosses towards her.

'You risked your life for me,' she says.

Lina looks up at her. '*You* risked your life for *us*,' she says.

'That was different,' Belle tells her. 'That was my robot protocol at work.'

And I see Lina smile. 'That was my *human* protocol at work,' she says.

Belle smiles back.

Then she reaches down to Lina. Lina returns her pulser to her belt and takes Belle's hand, and Belle pulls her to her feet. The two of them are looking into one another's eyes. Then, at exactly the same moment, they both utter a single word.

'Thanks.'

The atmosphere is triumphant.

'Bring it on!' Tex is shouting. 'We're scavengers! We won't be defeated!'

And the others whoop and cheer.

I know just how they're feeling. We've done it! With a mixture of cunning and bravery, we zilched the invading zoids. Every single one of them. And, for our pains, we've got a mass of gleaming zoid wreckage that'll keep us in parts for a long time to come.

The thing is though, it isn't over yet. Not by a long way. According to Belle, internal alarms in the zilched zoids have already alerted others back in the Outer Hull, and it won't be long before a second attack is launched.

'We need to clear away those zoids,' I tell the others. 'Get the transporter doors locked and sealed . . .'

'*They* need to do that,' Belle tells me, nodding to Lina, Dek and the others. '*We* need to get back to Zone 8. Dextra should have repaired the life-pods by now.'

Lina's overheard us. I see her frown and expect her to object to us setting off on our own again. But something in her seems to have changed. She still might not like Belle, but she has a new respect for her. More importantly, she seems to trust her.

'We have to return to the memory banks of the Core and finish this thing once and for all,' I explain to her.

And Lina nods and smiles and takes both my hands in hers. 'I know,' she says. She squeezes my hands warmly. 'I'll be waiting for you when you've succeeded.'

I smile back. Lina sounds a lot more sure about

me than I do about myself.

'Take care, York,' she says, and lets me go. 'Take care, both of you.'

Belle and I head back through the Mediterranean zone towards Zone 8 as quickly as we can. With the power still out, the walkways are not moving. But we make good progress over the scrubby terrain, passing between wild olives, cork oaks and shaggy pine trees. Birds perch in their branches. Goats graze in their shade. And the warm air is filled with the smell of orange blossom and thyme . . .

'There it is,' says Belle, pointing ahead at the cluster of low buildings that form the main complex of the lab zone.

Minutes later we're entering the underground lab. Dextra is there, stooped over one of the life-pods. And beside her, seated at a table and staring into its holo-panel, I'm surprised to see Cronos. He looks weary. There are dark shadows beneath his eyes and his tunic is stained with gunk-juice and scorch marks.

When he notices us, he smiles. 'York, Belle,' he says, 'you did well.'

He nods towards the schematic of the Mid Deck glowing in the air in front of him.

'Transporters 1 and 2 are secured,' he says. 'We isolated and decommissioned all the contaminated droids. And we've identified and sealed off the ventilation ducts that they used to transmit those sonic sound waves, but . . .' He sighs and wipes a hand over his grimy forehead. 'But I'm more convinced than ever that all this was just a preliminary assault,' he tells us. 'The zoids were simply testing our defences. The next attack will be the real thing—'

'The life-pods have been repaired,' Dextra breaks in, turning and looking at Belle, then at me. 'You can return to the Core now. But Cronos is right,' she says. 'The zoids will be back. And if you don't find the glitch before they overrun the Mid Deck, I can't promise you'll have bodies to return to.'

I shudder when I think of those zombified humans stumbling out of the transporters.

Belle steps forward. 'We have to return through the memory banks all the way to the Launch Times,' she announces. 'That way we can follow Samuel Marston, owner of the bad Mark unit, right through his life until we find what triggered the glitch.'

She turns to me and takes my hand.

'But I have to warn you, York,' Belle tells me. 'To get that far back as fast as possible, we will have to freefall through the fractal maze.'

I have no idea what that means – and I'm not sure I like the sound of it.

'If that's the only way,' I say, attempting a smile.

The others are watching us.

'Belle nods. 'It is,' she says.

# 29

I'm nervous. There's no point trying to hide it.

Dextra's told me that, in the event of another zoid attack on the Mid Deck, my mind might not be able to return to my body. Belle's warned me about this so-called fractal maze we have to take. Hot swarf! As though the first journey back into the memory bank wasn't weird and dangerous and frightening enough, now this!

So I'm lying here in the black pod, eyes closed, waiting for the lid to be shut. And I'm scared.

Of course, I'm putting on a brave face. When Dextra asks if I'm all right, I tell her I'm just fine. But the monitors I'm hooked up to tell a different story.

'Heartbeat fast. Blood pressure raised. Perspiration levels high,' Dextra intones. 'York,' she says, 'you can't go down into the memory banks in this state. I could give you something to calm you down, but—'

'No,' says Belle, her voice coming from the pod next to mine. 'York's mind must be clear if we're to navigate the memory banks successfully.'

'But with levels of stress this high,' says Dextra, 'you

might not even get that far . . .'

'We cannot *not* go,' says Belle.

'Belle's right,' Cronos chips in. 'There is no alternative.'

'I don't advise it,' says Dextra firmly.

I listen to them arguing over me. I don't know what to do or say. Of course I must return to the memory banks. But if my mental state means that I'll be useless there, then what's the point? And I'm wondering whether there's anything I can do to calm myself down, when I feel something tickle my ear.

I reach up and scratch it. The tickling continues, and I hear a kind of soft slurping noise. My eyes snap open – to see a small furry face pressed into mine.

'Caliph!' I exclaim.

The little skeeter jumps onto my chest, then leans down and licks my nose. I reach up, not caring whether I dislodge the sensors from my skin. It is so good to see him again.

'How've you been, eh, Caliph, boy?' I ask him, ruffling the fur behind his ears and stroking his back till he chitters and purrs with pleasure.

The last time I saw him was just

before I went down into the memory banks the first time. He was sitting up on Dextra's shoulders.

'You're looking good,' I say, as the little critter squirms about in my hands. 'Dextra's been looking after you, has she?'

I look up, to see that the others are staring down at me, smiles on their faces. Even Belle's.

'I feel a bit better now,' I say sheepishly.

'So I can see,' says Dextra happily, her wings smoothly folded at her shoulders. She gestures towards the monitor screens. 'And all ready to go. Come on, Caliph,' she says, reaching down and taking him from me. 'I'll keep looking after him,' she reassures me.

'I know you will,' I say. 'I'll be back before you know it,' I tell Caliph. 'Be a good boy.'

And the little skeeter jumps up onto Dextra's shoulders between her wings, where he chirrups back at me like he's understood.

Cronos stands up from the table and crosses the lab to the pods.

'Good luck,' he says as he closes first Belle's pod, then mine.

As the lids click into place, I close my eyes again. I'm feeling different now, excited rather than daunted by the task that lies ahead.

What *will* it be like to freefall down a fractal maze?

It's not like before, that's for certain. Not at all.

The other times there was white-out and then suddenly I was somewhere else. A place I recognized. But not this time. No. This time I'm just falling and falling and falling . . .

Belle's beside me.

There's nothing for my mind to hold on to. No ladder. No rungs.

We're inside this long glowing white tunnel that's twisting and turning in the air as we plummet. It's like being inside a whirlwind, the air warm and whistling. My head's spinning and my stomach's clenched.

So *this* is what it means to be in blind freefall.

Suddenly the white turns to green. Countless ribbons of luminous light pour through the air in an endless waterfall of digital flow. Data in shimmering constellations.

It's like some fantastically complicated series of equations. And we're in the middle of them.

Tube-surfing's fast, but this is so much faster. And

weirder. It feels like everything around us is expanding at a fantastic rate, creating pulsing eddies and spinning spirals, and great bulging spheres that grow and grow, then bud and burst out in new directions. The eddies and spirals repeat and repeat, and the spheres bud and burst, bud and burst, over and over again.

It's fantastically beautiful. Colours shimmer like oil on water. Shapes bend and fold.

I look down.

Belle has all but disappeared. It's as though the swirling fractals have soaked into her body, and instead of seeing her, all I can see is a Belle-shaped outline in the multicoloured patterns.

I hold a hand up in front of my face. And it's the same. Just an outline, falling through the dazzling, pulsing, flashing display . . .

Hot swarf!

For a moment panic starts to rise within me. I have nothing to hold on to. No sense of space. No sense of time. I feel totally lost – a random thought in an infinite maze of data . . .

But then I feel a hand close around mine. Belle's hand. I hear her voice.

'Hold on, York,' she tells me. 'Don't let go . . .'

Even as I hear these words though, I feel my grip on this virtual hand start to loosen. My thought-generated

fingers
begin to
slip, one
imagined finger
at a time . . .
'Don't let go . . .'
The fractal maze
convulses around
me as I fall through it.
Without Belle's hand, I
would be lost. Utterly lost.
A black hole opens up below us and light pours into
it like water down a plughole. I look down at the swirling
vortex, terrified by the thought of getting sucked inside.
But Belle has other ideas. I suddenly feel her hand tug
mine, and we disappear down into it.

# 31

I'm in a large hangar-like construction with a curved visiglass wall at each end. Beyond these walls, floating in space, are hundreds of engineers, hard at work. Close by, three robots are holding a great semicircular section of metal steady, while a man dressed in an orange spacesuit and visiglass helmet rivets it into place. Beyond them a gang of humans and robots are assembling what I guess must be the great nuclear-fusion engine.

I'm looking out at the construction of the Biosphere.

'This is back before Year Zero,' I hear Belle say.

I turn. She's there beside me in this holographic recording of the past, stored deep in the memory banks of the Core.

'So we made it through the fractal maze,' I say.

'We did. Your mind is strong, York,' she tells me. 'Stronger than I'd dared hope.'

I smile. It's good to have her by my side.

'We don't have much time,' she goes on. 'We need to find Marston. But as usual you'll have to be careful not to cause ripples that the virus scanners can pick up.'

I look round, taking in the construction work. Apart from a rib-like series of curved beams, the Biosphere is little more than the Inner Core right now, and even that hasn't been completed. On the far right of this orbiting building site is a docked space-jet, with a line of robots unloading parts from the hold. And heading in our direction, their vapour trails making them look like shooting stars, are two more of the space-jets, towing vast bundles of urilium scaffolding behind them.

It's awesome. All of it.

Suddenly my gaze falls on a figure in a green-and-white jumpsuit. He's standing on a raised steel platform at the end of the hangar. I recognize his gaunt face at once.

'There! There!' I exclaim.

Marston's head is down, and he's working on some kind of palm-computer that's glowing in his hand.

'Well done, York,' says Belle. 'I'm going to try and put a digi-marker on him,' she tells me. 'But first you need to be connected to me.'

She puts a holo-band around my wrist. I see she is also wearing one. They glow white as they sync.

'Think of these as portable mind-ladders,'

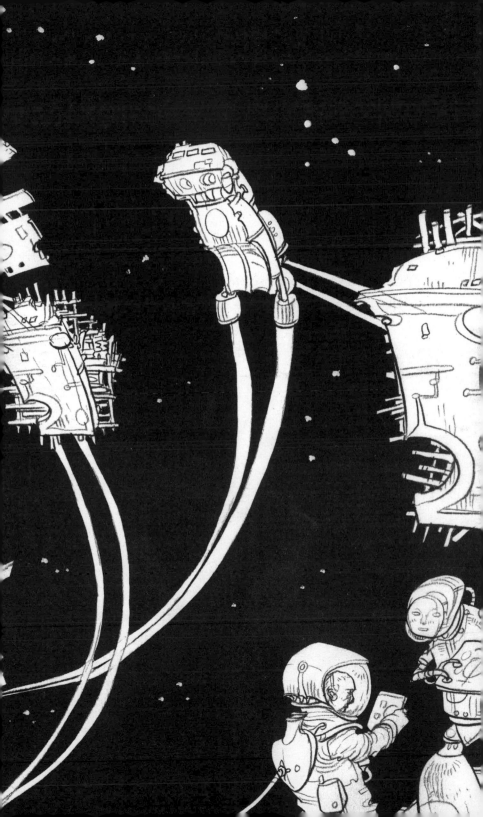

she tells me. 'We've got to be ready to move quickly through the memory banks because every time-jump we

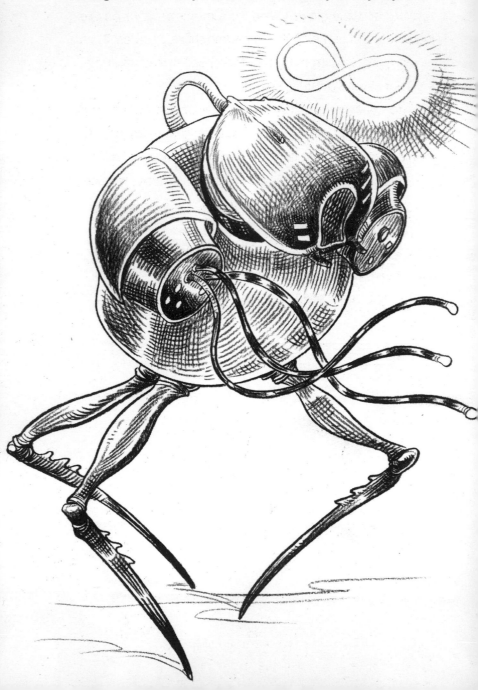

make will cause a ripple in the data-stream.'

As I watch her, Belle's eyes glaze over, her head falls forward and she glows green for a moment. Over on the ledge Marston himself pulses the same shade of green. Then, as the glow fades from both of them, Belle looks up at me.

'That should do it,' she says.

And not a moment too soon, because just then a virus-scanner zoid appears. It comes speeding towards us, the infinity symbol above its head shining brightly.

The band at my wrist glows white. Belle takes my hand once more, her grip ferociously tight.

The scene in front of us dissolves into a pixelated blur. A moment later the scrambled images come back together and the scene sharpens into focus.

'Launch Year Zero,' Belle says.

# 32

We're at the centre of a broad, wedge-shaped room on the viewing deck of the Biosphere, surrounded by hundreds of people. The atmosphere is one of almost uncontrolled excitement.

Belle lets go of my hand. The pair of us scan the place, trying to take it all in.

The floor is terraced, and above our heads the ceiling panels glow milky white. Three of the walls have sliding doors set into them, which keep opening and closing as more and more people pour into the already crammed room. The fourth wall is a huge tinted visiglass window. A jostling crowd of men and women are pressed up against it, staring out.

The place is brand spanking new. Everything is polished and shiny. The air smells of fresh polysynth and nyoprene and hot electric wiring. Gleaming workstations with computer decks and holo-screens are set up in rows, ten to a terrace. There's a person seated at every one, operating the controls – and with another nine or ten people clustered around each of them, watching, pointing, chattering noisily.

Raised above them all is a master control pod, where two men are sitting side by side in reclining moulded seats. There's a glimmer of green coming from one of them.

'Marston,' says Belle.

I nod. And I recognize the man next to him as well. It's Atherton, the chief engineer. Alive and well.

Their holo-screen has a time display on it – a row of zeroes that haven't even started moving yet.

'Activate departure protocol,' Atherton says into the

microphone unit clamped to his collar, and his voice is amplified throughout the viewing deck.

Everyone takes a sharp breath. Computer operatives leap into action.

It's time.

Belle grabs my hand and we pick our way through the crowd, taking care not to walk through anything or anyone.

'Prepare life-support transfer,' Atherton instructs as we reach the viewing window.

There's another flurry of activity all around us. A babble of voices. People are holding hands, smiles on their faces and eyes unblinking as they stare ahead through the tinted visiglass screen. Belle and I slip between them, till the two of us are right at the front, with a perfect view outside.

And I gasp.

Below me is the planet Earth. The Biosphere is in orbit above it.

It's nothing like the pictures of Earth that I saw in the vid-streams when I was a boy. This is no blue-and-green planet. It's grey and brown. The sea is like a vast expanse of rusty corrugated iron; while the land is dark and dead, apart from the huge fires that are burning out of control, destroying the last of the forests and turning the immense cities to smoking rubble.

'Engage thrust rockets.'

There are people down there, I realize. For though the Great War has wiped out huge swathes of the population, and the Pestilence still more, millions, possibly billions still remain. And a painful lump forms in my throat that I cannot swallow away, as I think of what it must be like being one of them, looking up at the Biosphere, as the chosen ones from Earth are about to depart and leave them to their terrible fate.

'Commence countdown,' Atherton announces calmly, and his hand passes over a holo-dial set into the arm of his chair.

'Ten . . . nine . . . eight . . .'

A mechanical voice starts counting, only to be drowned out by the human voices that join in. Hundreds of them. Loud, and getting louder.

'*Six! . . . Five! . . . Four! . . .*'

I hear the roar of the engines starting up. And through the floor I sense a deep vibrating rumble rise from the centre of the Biosphere, this great man-made planet that carries with it the future of humanity.

'*Three! . . . Two! . . .*'

Most of the faces I see are laughing and smiling. But there are others who feel as I do. Distraught. Frightened. Maybe their loved ones are already dead. Maybe they've been forced to leave them behind. Tears are streaming down their faces, and their bodies shake as they sob.

'*ONE! . . .*'

But it's too late now. Everything is ready. Years of preparation have been completed, and the time has come for the Biosphere to leave the dying Earth and set off across the galaxies on a journey to a new planet.

The time display in front of Marston starts moving, showing the passing of the first seconds on board the newly launched Biosphere.

Year 0. 00-00. 00:00:01 . . . 00:00:02 . . . 03 . . .

*'DEPART EARTH'S ORBIT!'*

All at once, the sound of the engine rises in pitch, the spaceship trembles and as the Biosphere accelerates. On the other side of the visiglass window, the Earth shrinks at incredible speed as we leave its orbit and rocket out into the blackness beyond. Seconds later it's the size of a gunkball. Seconds after that, a rusty rivet.

Then it's gone.

People are laughing and crying and hugging one another.

'We're on our way!' they're shouting.

'Farewell, Earth!'

I turn to Belle. She is staring over at Marston, and I notice that the Mark unit is now standing beside him. It's time to follow the two of them, to find out exactly when the glitch in the robot's protocol occurred.

The holo-band around my wrist glows white. Belle takes my hand once more.

'Ready, York?' she says.

'Ready,' I say.

# 33

Launch Year 12. Samuel Marston is thirty-eight years old.

As the green glow of the digi-marker fades, I see he is biting into a peach. His dumpy personal-help robot has just picked it from the tree growing in the hydroponic grow-trough beside them.

'Life is good,' Marston mutters, wiping the juice from his mouth.

The robot pulls a recliner across the floor and positions it behind Marston.

'If you would like to sit down, sir,' it says, its voice mechanical but friendly.

Marston does so, and sighs. '*Very* good,' he says.

A young woman walks past, a sleek robot attendant gliding after her. She pauses beside the recliner.

'Relaxing, Mission Commander?' she asks, and her pale blue eyes sparkle. 'That's a Robotic Assist-Level Personal Help, if I'm not mistaken.'

'A Mark 1,' says Marston, nodding.

'It's *so* Launch Year Zero,' she says.

'*He*,' Marston corrects her.

'I've upgraded to a far superior model,' she tells him. 'And you should too. A man of your importance.'

Marston climbs to his feet, the half-eaten peach in his hand. He gives it back to his robot, who offers him a rather grubby-looking towel in return.

'Mark 1 here and I go back a long way,' Marston says. 'Of course he's not the brightest diode in the motherboard. Are you, Mark?'

'Sir?' says Mark.

'I'd only had him a week when he did that to himself.' Marston laughs and points at the scratch and dent on the robot's head. 'Fell off a hover-bike, didn't you, Mark?'

'I did, sir,' says Mark amiably.

Marston sighs. 'But he's an old friend, Engineer . . .' He frowns. 'What did you say your name was?'

'I didn't,' she says. 'You can call me Delphine.'

# 34

Launch Year 27. Samuel Marston is fifty-three.

His cheeks have hollowed out and there are dark rings around his eyes. He's hunched over a holo-screen in a cluttered study-room. Stacks of bio-samples lean against the walls. Info-disks, tech-pads and data files are strewn across the floor beside discarded clothes and half-finished bev snacks.

There's a soft swooshing noise as a door slides open, and I have to smile as Mark waddles into the room on his stubby legs, liquid slopping from the small visiglass cup he's

holding. He's so cute – just like the Ralph unit that saved my life back in the Outer Hull.

'It is time for your medicine, sir,' he says.

Marston rolls his eyes, but takes the cup and downs the thick white liquid in one gulp. Then he pats Mark on his dome-shaped head.

'Thanks, old friend,' he says.

The door slides open again, and Delphine strides into the room. She looks concerned.

'You can't go on like this, Sammy,' she says. 'Working all hours. I never get to see you.'

'I know, but—' Marston begins, climbing to his feet.

'You *said* we'd work as a team,' Delphine breaks in. 'You *promised* . . .'

'You don't understand,' Marston tells her. 'I'm responsible for the safe running of the Biosphere—'

'And look at this place,' she goes on. 'Everything's moved on, yet you're still living in Launch Year Zero.'

'It's all fine, Delphine,' Marston tells her wearily. 'Once I've worked my way through this latest batch—'

'And as for *that* thing, it just about sums it all up,' she says, rounding on the little robot. 'I mean, *look* at it!'

'How may I serve you?' Mark asks her, his stumpy arms waving about.

Delphine rolls her eyes. 'I've been saying for years

you should get an upgrade. You're mission commander, Sammy. You deserve—'

Marston slams a fist on his desk, sending a pile of info-discs clattering to the floor.

'Stop nagging me!' he says sharply. 'I don't need an upgraded robot. I'm happy with the way things are. I—'

'But *I'm* not, Samuel,' Delphine says. 'I can't live this way any longer – which is why I've taken a new post in the Mid Deck. Zone 3.'

Her pale eyes gleam.

'It's got to be better than being here every day, watching you destroy yourself.'

She falls still. Marston cannot meet her gaze.

'If that's the way you want it,' he says calmly.

He sits back down and returns his attention to the graphs and formulae and data-streams on the holo-screen. Delphine watches him for a moment, then turns and heads from the room. Marston slumps back in his chair. He looks worse than ever.

Beside him, Mark sets down the pile of info-discs he has picked up from the floor.

'Your work, sir,' he says.

Marston looks at the little robot and smiles. 'Ah, Mark,' he says softly, 'at least *you* understand me.'

Launch Year 29. Marston is fifty-five.

He's standing beside a bed, and I'm surprised to see who's lying in it. It's Delphine. And she looks awful. Sweaty, feverish, her clammy skin as white as the bedcovers draped over her.

Marston is holding one of her bony hands in his own.

'I just can't bear to think of you gone,' he is saying. 'Please reconsider, Delphine. I'm begging you . . .'

'No, Sammy,' she says, her voice weak but determined.

'Oh, Delphine.' He sounds desperate. 'What can I say to make you change your mind?'

'Nothing, Sammy,' she tells him. Then she smiles. 'You must let me go . . .'

And with that, she closes her eyes.

Marston bows his head. There are tears at the corners of his eyes.

'I don't want to live without you, Delphine,' he says quietly. 'If *you* won't have yourself uploaded into a mind-tomb, then neither shall I. Ever.'

At the far side of the sick-pod, the door slides open. Mark enters, a box in his hands.

'My condolences, sir,' he says.

Marston turns to him. 'What are those?' he asks.

'Tissues, sir,' Mark says. 'To dry your tears should you weep or sob . . .'

For a moment Marston does not move. Then he kneels down, takes the box of tissues and places them on the ground.

'Oh, Mark,' he says, his voice cracking with emotion, and he wraps his arms around the little robot's dumpy body. 'I've lost her.'

Mark's eyes flash on and off. His mouthpiece buzzes. Then, as I watch, I see one stumpy arm patting Marston awkwardly on the shoulder.

'It's just you and me now, Mark, old friend,' says Marston. 'Just you and me.'

# 36

Launch Year 42. Marston is sixty-eight.

He's standing next to a trolley, wearing only a towel wrapped around his middle. His shoulders are slumped; his body is stooped. He seems to be having some kind of medical check-up. Two anxious-looking young bio-technicians are fussing about him.

'What is all this nonsense anyway?' Marston says grumpily.

'The latest advance,' one of them tells him, then turns to a droid. 'Commence molecular scan.'

'At once, sir,' says the droid, beams of light streaming from its eyes. Marston's body is bathed in blue, while a single red dot flickers quickly across his wrinkled skin. 'Molecular scan complete,' it says moments later.

'So, what's the result?' Marston says, turning to the second bio-engineer, who has moved across to a bank of holo-screens.

'There's some inflammation in the knee joints,' she says. 'And the elbows. And—'

'Minor aches and pains,' Marston interrupts. 'I could

have told you that . . . Sophie,' he says, squinting at her
name badge. 'How much longer do I have to live?'

Sophie smiles. 'Judging by these results, Mission Commander, you'll live to be a hundred.'

Marston sighs. 'I'm not sure I want to live that long,' he says. 'Now that the younger generation has everything under control, I'm not needed any more . . .'

'Oh, you mustn't say that, sir,' Sophie tells him earnestly. 'You are our link with the Earth. You lived upon it. Swam in its oceans. Walked through its forests . . .' She swallows unhappily. 'Me, I've never even *seen* it.'

'Maybe,' says Marston. 'But I also saw what humans did to the Earth. The wars. The destruction . . .'

'Which is why we need you,' Sophie persists. 'So we don't make the same mistakes again.'

Marston shrugs.

'Please don't get me wrong, sir,' Sophie goes on. 'I hope you don't go into a mind-tomb for many years.' She pauses. 'But when you do, then you will be able to guide us. Forever . . .'

I see the flash of horror that crosses Marston's face.

'But for now,' she continues, 'you can pop your clothes back on.'

Marston nods. 'Mark,' he calls.

The roly-poly robot – still 'good' so far as I can see – comes waddling towards him from behind a screen. His arms are outstretched, with clothes hanging over them. But then, as he reaches Marston, he trips, stumbles and the clothes drop to the floor.

'Oh dear,' he says.

'Never mind, Mark,' says Marston softly, reaching down to pick up his shirt. 'Thank you for your help.'

He doesn't notice the two bio-engineers exchanging glances behind his back.

'That thing's hopelessly outdated,' the man mutters, shaking his head.

Sophie frowns. 'The mission commander is emotionally attached to it,' she whispers. 'Where's the harm in that?'

# 37

Launch Year 47. Samuel Marston is seventy-three.

He is sitting on a stool at the far end of a vast hall, in front of a mind-tomb. David Atherton's glowing face is looking down at him. The pair of them are playing chess. It's Marston's move, but he is deep in his own thoughts.

'What's it like, Atherton?' he asks at last.

Around the two of them, standing in rows on the black marble floor, are other mind-tombs. Crew members are standing in front of some of them, and the air is filled with a soft babble of voices as the living members of the Biosphere communicate with the Half-Lifes.

'You ask me that every time we play,' says Atherton.

'It's something I want to understand,' says Marston. '*Need* to understand.'

'It's a bit like daydreaming. Only more real . . . Sometimes I'll go to touch something, and have to remind myself I can't.' He pauses. 'Your move, Samuel.'

Marston nods. Moves a pawn.

'It's a time for contemplation,' Atherton continues. 'For endless meditation about yourself . . .'

'And others?' says Marston.

'When crew members ask my advice, I am there for them,' says Atherton. 'I like to think I have helped.'

Marston nods thoughtfully. 'And the other Half-Lifes?' he says. 'You communicate with them?'

'Yes,' says Atherton. 'We share our knowledge, our wisdom, our memories of our past experiences . . .' He pauses. 'Rook takes bishop,' he says, and Mark moves the holo-chess piece for him. 'Check.'

'Clever,' says Marston quietly. He falls still. I think he's mulling over his next move, but when he speaks his mind is still elsewhere. 'What does it *feel* like?'

Atherton's glowing face sighs. 'It's true, Samuel, there are downsides to being a Half-Life. You cannot taste or smell. Or touch. Then again, you're also free from all physical pain—'

'But what about the *mental* pain?' Marston breaks in. 'You don't know the thoughts I have. Such dark thoughts.'

He lowers his head. Atherton watches and listens, but this time he says nothing.

'They call me a genius. I understand why they want to upload my mind into a mind-tomb,' Marston goes on, 'but the thought of it continuing, forever . . . I'm telling you, David, it terrifies me.'

'You must have courage, Samuel,' says Atherton. 'We

need you. Especially now. The younger crew members have to learn what we know. Why we built the Biosphere. Why we had to leave Earth. They must not repeat the mistakes of the past.'

'You're right of course,' says Marston. 'But the thought still terrifies me. In fact, I've been thinking long and hard about . . .' He pauses, glances around at his little robot. 'Where do you think I should move next, Mark?' he asks.

'Perhaps knight to . . . errm . . . no . . . Bishop to . . .' His red eyes flash on and off. 'Yes, king's bishop to . . .'

'Oh, Mark, Mark, Mark . . .' Marston chuckles softly. 'You still haven't got the hang of it, have you?'

'Thinking long and hard about what?' asks Atherton.

'Oh, nothing,' Marston mutters, and I know he's still imagining his consciousness continuing after he dies. Forever. 'Queen takes rook,' he says, then sits back and folds his arms. 'Checkmate.'

Launch Year 58. Marston is eighty-four years old.

He and Sophie, the bio-engineer I saw back at the medical examination room, are walking arm in arm. Marston is holding a walking stick in his free hand, and Mark is waddling along at his side.

He *still* looks 'good'.

The three of them are on the path that winds its way between the hydroponic grow-troughs. The fruit trees are neatly pruned, their trunks much thicker than when I last saw them.

'You're like the daughter I never had, Sophie,' Marston is saying to her, his voice weak and faltering. 'And you remind me so much of her . . .'

'Who?' Sophie asks.

'Of Delphine,' he tells her.

'Ah, yes,' she says. 'Didn't you tell me she once worked here?'

'I did,' says Marston, and he smiles, his head full of memories. 'I loved her.'

They continue strolling between the trees, the sunlight

units warm and bright overhead. Marston nods towards one of the lens-head droids, busy gathering samples of blossom from an orange tree.

'It's incredible how . . .' he begins.

But then he stumbles. His stick clatters to the ground and he just stands there staring down at it, his face drained of all colour. Mark waddles forward, picks it up and returns it to Marston – but not before Sophie has noticed how badly the old man's hand is shaking.

'How long have you had that tremor?' she asks him.

Marston looks at his hand as though seeing it for the first time.

'This?' he says. 'A while now. But it doesn't bother me.' He laughs weakly. 'I've always been clumsy. And anyway, Mark here helps me out. Don't you, Mark?'

'My aim is to serve you, sir,' the dumpy robot says, which makes Sophie laugh.

'I always forget how polite these old droids are,' she says.

'He's been with me my whole working life,' Marston tells her. 'Call me a sentimental old fool, but I can't bear the thought of being without him.'

Sophie pats his hand. 'You're not a fool, Mission Commander,' she says. 'You're the wisest man I know. And none of us could do without you.' She links arms with him again. 'Now, if you'd just let me run a few tests . . .'

# 39

Launch Year 67. Marston is ninety-three.

We're watching Mark tidy a sleep-pod in some kind of medi-centre room. Cleaning, ordering, putting away.

In the corner, the green glow of the digi-marker fades, and Marston glides forward. He is in a robotic walker, strapped upright to a rigid backboard, staring at a holo-keyboard projected just in front of his immobile face. As his eyes move, a mechanical voice speaks.

'Mark,' it drones, 'stop doing that. I need your help.'

'How may I serve you, sir?' the little robot responds as he waddles obediently over to Marston's side.

'There isn't much time,' the mechanical voice says. 'Sophie will be here soon to take me to the ceremony. They want to upload me into a mind-tomb – and I can't let that happen. So you will have to help me, old friend.'

'How may I serve you, sir?' Mark repeats.

'Show me your protocol access key,' Marston says.

'My protocol access key is restricted, sir.'

'Mission-commander override,' the old man's mechanical voice intones. 'Marston double-helix eight.'

'Mission-commander override in need of dual-verification, sir,' says Mark.

'Dual-verification . . .' He pauses. 'Atherton double-helix four.'

'Override accepted,' says Mark, and projects a glowing circular disc into the air.

It is covered in a grid across which streams of data are moving in intricate patterns. Another disc follows it, then another and another. Soon the air between the robot and the paralysed Marston is filled with a constellation of spinning discs.

Marston stares at them unblinking. He seems to be searching for something in particular as they orbit around him – until one comes to a halt directly in front of his eyes.

I feel Belle tense beside me.

'Primary protocol accessed,' says Mark. 'But I must warn you, any alteration will affect my safe functioning.'

Marston stares hard at the disc, then blinks twice.

I see a single line of data detach itself from the surface of the disc and fall, symbol by symbol, down through the air before vanishing. I turn to Belle. She is staring at the space where the symbols just disappeared. Her eyes glow white for a moment, then fade to their usual green.

'Is that the glitch we've been searching for?' I whisper.

'Not a glitch,' Belle replies, 'but a deliberate act of sabotage. Marston has made it possible for the robot to

harm him. It is against the first law of robotics.' She pauses. 'This is the moment. Good Mark has been turned bad.'

I shake my head. 'Marston didn't realize,' I say. 'He wanted to end his own life. That was all . . .'

'The robots communicate among themselves,' says Belle. 'We know that. If Mark harms Marston, then no human will ever be safe again.'

I look back at the scene before us.

'Activate amended protocol,' Marston commands.

Mark shuts off the projection. The spinning discs disappear.

'Thank you, old friend,' says Marston, the mechanical voice betraying no emotion. 'Now, before you deactivate yourself, you can do me one last kindness.'

'How may I serve you, sir?' Mark asks.

'Let me die.'

Mark looks at the life-support system he has deactivated, then at his master. Samuel Marston is still strapped into the robotic walker. He is not moving. Not at all. But there is the trace of a smile on his lips.

Red eyes flashing, Mark switches the system back on.

The control unit hums into action, and lights on the display panel flicker. Waddling closer, Mark confirms no signs of life are being displayed on any of the holo-screens. Heartbeat. Pulse. Brain activity . . . The digital blip on every one has flatlined.

Mark takes a step back. Then, with a soft bleep, he deactivates himself. The glowing red eyes switch off. His head slumps forward.

And I realize there's a lump in my throat.

The little robot, Mark, has gone. And by his own hand. Down the years, I watched him being so helpful to Marston. So loyal. So dependable. So kind. Sure, he made mistakes. Spilling stuff. Knocking things over. But somehow that just made him seem all the more human.

He'd never wanted to harm humans, only to serve

them. He'd warned Marston about tampering with his protocol, aware that it would affect his ability to function safely. Even after he had been turned 'bad', he still tried to do the right thing. That was why he shut himself down. No, whatever happened later, it was certainly not the fault of the Robotic-Assist Level Personal Help Mark 1 unit.

Not that it softens the horror of what happened later, when the robots rebelled . . .

Just then, interrupting my thoughts, the door slides open and Sophie enters the room. She hurries over to the walker.

'Oh, Samuel!' she exclaims, and turns

to the black-robed attendants who have followed her in. 'It's no good,' she sobs. 'We're too late.'

One of the attendants looks across at Mark. 'Haven't seen one of them in years,' he says.

Sophie looks up, tears in her eyes. 'This robot was a faithful servant to the mission commander,' she says. 'It looked after him all his life. Now that Samuel is dead, its own purpose has gone. Make sure you store it away carefully.' Her tearful voice catches in her throat. 'It's . . . it's what Samuel would have wanted.'

I feel Belle tug on my sleeve.

'We need to get out of here,' she says. 'Before a virus scanner picks us up.'

'Back to the fractal maze?' I say.

Belle shakes her head. 'No, York. We can't risk that a second time. Your mind might not be up to it,' she says. 'I'm going to construct the mind-ladder again.'

As she speaks, familiar ripples of white light appear at my feet.

'Follow me,' Belle says.

# 41

Climbing down the mind-ladder was hard. Climbing up it is harder.

Infinitely harder.

All around me are pulsing, writhing data-streams. Some whine or hiss as they flow past; others make the ladder judder as they whoosh by. I look up. The ladder stretches off above me, seemingly forever.

'Focus on one rung at a time.'

It's Belle's voice, calling up to me. She's close behind me, but sounds so far away.

'I'm trying to get us up through the Core's central pathway as quickly as possible,' she's saying. 'But we've been so deep inside the memory banks that it's hard to keep the mind-ladder in focus . . .'

And as she speaks, the air turns to a shade of deepest blue. Then from blue to indigo. Then indigo to

black. It throbs around me. It presses in from all sides. Darkness seems to be billowing up towards us like a dense fog. There is twinkling in the inky blackness. Pulses of energy. Flashes of light . . .

It's the infinity symbols, I realize with a start. The Lazy 8s. The virus scanners.

Suddenly, out of the inky darkness, huge black tentacles emerge and probe the air. One of them winds itself around Belle.

'I must protect the data-memory,' she calls to me. She sounds urgent, but there is no trace of fear in her voice. 'Protect it in any way I can . . .'

I want to ask her what that means. But before I can, she's plucked clean away.

And now it's me the tentacles are coming after. One of them grabs my left leg. Another my right. They pull, hard, harder. I grip desperately onto the rungs. But one hand is tugged away and I'm left dangling. Then the tentacles start to prise the fingers of my remaining hand away from the metal rung, one by one, until . . .

I give up. Let go. There's nothing else I can do. And as the tentacles tighten their grip around my body, I'm dragged down into the empty blackness far below.

# 42

I'm nowhere. Lost. Alone . . .

There are no sounds. No smells. No tastes. There is nothing to see, nothing to touch. I have no sense of movement, or balance, or time, or space, or speed. Just this infinite emptiness that surrounds my consciousness – my *self*.

All I have is my thoughts.

I'm five years old again, back in my sleep-pod, at the Inpost in the Outer Hull. The lights are off, and I'm alone with the darkness, my mind playing tricks on me. There are demons in the lockers. There are monsters under the bed.

Except it's worse than that here. Far worse.

Back then I could snuggle up under the covers and pull the pillow over my head. Here, now, there's nothing to hold on to. I'm on my own. And in this endless nothingness, shouting out doesn't work either. It can't. I have no voice. No matter how loud I scream, there is only silence.

I flap my arms. I kick my legs. I move my hand around

in front of my face – which is when I see the faint light glowing and remember the holo-band that Belle secured around my wrist . . .

Belle!

My friend Belle, with her bobbed black hair and piercing green eyes. The two of us have been through so much together.

Where is she now?

I find myself thinking of all the times she's saved my life. Killing the monstrous worm-like critters in the chimney-vents of the Outer Hull . . . Pulling me from the deadly mud in one of the Mid Deck zones . . . Rescuing me from the clutches of the mind-warp monster that attacked me in the Core . . .

Memory after memory comes flooding back. It's good to have something for my mind to hold on to in this dark emptiness. I concentrate harder. On her – on Belle. And, as I do, the holo-band at my wrist glows brighter.

I remember how intently she sometimes looks at me, trying to understand my emotions. Happiness, sadness, anger and all the rest. Little by little she is learning to feel the way that humans feel, and I am her teacher . . .

The holo-band glows brighter still.

Then, far in the distance, I catch sight of a second light. It's dim and faltering.

I remember Belle's first smile. The first joke we shared. The first tear she shed . . .

The light grows brighter as it comes nearer. It's like I'm drawing it towards me.

Truth is, I feel closer to Belle than to any human I've ever met. She's a zoid. But she's like no zoid I've ever known.

The light gets bigger, brighter, closer.

Loyal. Brave. Intuitive . . .

,

And closer still.

Selfless. Caring . . .

The light is hovering before me now. It's the second holo-band, the one around Belle's wrist, glowing as intensely bright as my own. By thinking about my friend, I've brought her back to me. I reach out. There is a flash, and the dazzling glow from the two holo-bands becomes one as we clasp each other's hands and hold on tightly.

My friend Belle.

My words are silent. I only hope she knows what I'm thinking.

# 43

I'm still nowhere. And lost. But at least I'm not alone any more. Belle is with me. It makes the nothingness a bit more bearable.

I don't know how long we've been floating in the empty darkness when I see it. Another far- off speck of glowing light. As I watch, this tiny light grows steadily brighter.

Belle's seen it too.

The light draws closer to us and I see that it isn't a single point of light at all, but rather a constellation of glowing dots connected by a grid-like tracery of criss-crossing lines. As they come closer still, they form the outline of a single entity, made out of pure data.

It swims towards us with shimmering, pulsing wingbeats. There is something nightmarish about its slow graceful movement, getting closer and closer . . .

Suddenly the data-creature is right in front of us. The glowing grid seems to open up and we're being pulled inside it. Then with a sickening lurch, we're propelled into motion and sent hurtling down into a tunnel of swirling data, its sides blurring as we gather speed.

It's like tube-surfing again, but unimaginably fast.

Belle's still beside me and I grip hold of her wrist as hard as I can. There's no way I'm ever going to let go. But it isn't easy. As we keep on accelerating it feels like we're being pulled apart – which only makes me hold on all the more fiercely.

There's more light, far ahead of us. We're heading towards it. Then into it. Streaks of blurred light line the curve of the tunnel. Pinks and yellows.

Next to me, something extraordinary is happening to Belle. The pastel lights seem to be soaking into her until she too is glowing with the same soft colours. All apart from her eyes, that is. They're bright white, just like they were when she uploaded the data-memory. And as I watch, she blinks – once, twice, then so fast it's a blur – and suddenly, a panel of light appears at her chest, fizzing, pulsating.

She turns to me. Her eyes are green once more. She starts to speak – and I can hear her voice.

'The data-memory has been . . .'

But then it fades. The data-memory has been what?

The dawn light has become dazzlingly bright. Familiar

circles within circles of blinding whiteness speed towards us. Surround us. It's like all those other times when the white-out came and Belle reached into the portal she'd been holding open and pulled me to safety.

Except this time Belle is with me and there's nothing she can do.

# 44

'York? York.'

I open my eyes.

Belle is standing in front of me. The luminous light
is glowing in her chest panel – and everything comes
flooding back.

The void. The data-creature. The long, twisting tunnel
and . . .

'The data-memory,' I blurt out. 'Do you still have it?'

'I do,' Belle confirms, placing a hand on the panel. 'All
fixed, logged and safely uploaded here.'

'Thank the Half-Lifes for that,' I murmur. 'But where
are we?'

We seem to be in some immense space. Pillars of
light extend from a glowing floor up to a constellation of
shimmering fan vaults high above. It is spectacular and
beautiful, and I feel safe. Protected. The sound of voices
fills the air.

As my eyes slowly get used to the pulsing glow, I see
that there are figures all around us. The vertical shafts
of light are pouring down onto the tops of their heads,

making their bodies glow and pooling around their feet. I focus on one, then another, and as I do so, they become a little more distinct.

There's a woman in an old-style flight tunic. Two men in loose-fitting green robes. And then I see someone I recognize . . .

It's Atherton. David Atherton, chief engineer of the Launch Times. The first time I saw him was on the viewing deck of the Outer Hull. Then again when he was on the hover-stretcher, being uploaded into the mind-tomb, with Samuel Marston praising him as the person who'd made the Biosphere a success. Then, as a half life, playing chess . . .

Now here he is, walking towards me in a pool of golden light.

'Greetwell,' I say.

'Greetwell, York,' he replies, and he beams at me warmly, his glowing Half-Life face radiant. 'There is someone I would like you to meet.'

I turn, to see another golden shaft of light approaching.

'Bronx!' I exclaim.

'It's good to see you, York.' Bronx's glowing face smiles back at me. 'I told you we would meet in the Halls of Eternity.'

I look round. 'Is that where we are?' I say.

'It is,' says Bronx. 'Though you were in danger of being permanently deleted by the virus scanners,' he goes on. 'They detected your presence in the memory banks and tracked you down,' he says. 'Then they removed you from the Core into infinity – a digital void – where your consciousness would have unravelled and dissolved.' He pauses. 'Nothing personal.'

'Nothing personal?!' I exclaim.

'It's just the central computer protecting itself,' Bronx explains softly. 'It sealed itself off when the Rebellion in the Outer Hull began, and has been protecting the memory banks and guidance systems that are steering the Biosphere towards the new Earth ever since.' He smiles. 'We Half-Lifes are part of the Core,' he tells me. 'Where human memory lives on. We tracked you, and when you were cast adrift in the digital void, we were able to bring you here.'

'So we're safe?' I ask, looking around for glowing infinity symbols.

'None of us are safe,' Bronx says. 'The zoids' power is growing stronger all the time. They have constructed a central computer of their own in the Outer Hull that threatens to wipe out all trace of humanity – even our memories. By travelling in the memory banks, you and Belle have discovered what we have been searching for for so long.'

'The protocol.'

It is Atherton's voice. I turn to see him smiling at Belle.

'You understand the three laws of robotics?' he asks her. 'Created to ensure that robots would serve humans throughout our long journey.'

'I do,' says Belle. 'One, that a robot may not injure a human being or, through inaction, allow a human being to come to harm,' she replies. 'Two, that a robot must

211

obey orders given to it by a human being, except where such orders would conflict with the first law. And three, that a robot must protect its own existence – as long as that does not break the first two laws.'

Atherton is nodding. 'But there was also a fourth law. The robots were programmed to protect the Biosphere,' he tells her. 'And when Marston deleted the key bit of the primary protocol, robots no longer had to protect humans . . .'

'They only had to protect the Biosphere,' I breathe.

'Precisely,' says Bronx. 'They calculated that humans were a threat to the Biosphere. They saw them as an infestation to be exterminated to ensure the smooth running of the spaceship.'

'Poor Samuel,' Atherton says. 'If he'd realized the terrible consequences, he would never have done what he did.'

'Poor Samuel?!' says Bronx. 'Pah! Samuel Marston wasn't around to face those consequences, was he? That was left to the rest of us. All he was thinking about was himself – taking his own life rather than becoming a Half-Life. Or rather, altering the protocol of his robot to do it for him.' His glowing face pulsates with anger. 'If it wasn't for him—'

'If it wasn't for him, there would be no Biosphere,' Atherton interrupts softly. 'And I knew him, Bronx. It

would have torn him apart to know that that one small action of his would make everything go so wrong.'

Bronx looks as though he's going to say something else. But I speak first.

'So how do we put it right?'

Bronx turns his attention to me. His anger has melted away.

'You've got to get back to the Outer Hull and upload the protocol into the zoids' central computer,' he says. 'We have given Belle the exact coordinates. Once it is restored, the original robot protocol will spread throughout the zoids' network. And the Rebellion will end.'

It all sounds so easy. But we're in the Halls of Eternity. Scuzz only knows how we're going to get to the Outer Hull. But before I can ask, Bronx has stepped back, and I see him join the other glowing figures who have now formed a circle around us. Their light becomes brighter.

'Good luck,' says Bronx. 'I'm sure I don't have to tell you that the future of mankind depends on you.'

And I'm about to tell him we'll need a whole lot more than luck, when the glowing of the Half-Lifes intensifies, there's a deafening roaring in my ears and suddenly I'm travelling at the speed of light.

I'm back in the life-pod. I push open the lid – and Caliph's
on me at once, licking and slurping and slobbering all
over my face.

'Whoa, boy!' I say. 'I'm pleased to see you too!'

Dextra spins round from the info-stack she's standing
at, her wings trembling.

'You're back,' she says. 'Already.'

The lid of the pod next to me rises and Belle sits up.

'You're *both* back,' says Dextra. She looks distraught.
'What went wrong?'

'Nothing went wrong,' I say.

'So why are you back so quickly?' Dextra glances at
the scanner on her wrist. 'You've only been gone for ten
minutes.'

'Ten minutes!' I exclaim.

Caliph jumps back in alarm and scrambles up onto
one of the tech-stacks, chittering loudly.

'It felt like a lifetime,' I say, thinking of Samuel
Marston.

'We stepped outside time,' Belle says as she gets out

of her pod. 'In the Core we are just energy pulses. But we found what we needed.' She taps her chest panel. 'Now we have to act fast.'

Ten minutes. It's hard to take in. But at least it explains why I don't feel as disorientated as I did the last time I returned to the Mid Deck.

A second winged figure enters the room. It's Cronos. And if I needed any more proof that we weren't gone long, then here it is. He hasn't even had time to change out of that scorched and stained tunic of his.

'So how did it go?' he says

'We found the problem,' I tell him. 'And Belle knows what to do. But we have an even bigger problem. We need to return to the Outer Hull and find the zoids' central computer.'

'But, York,' Cronos says quietly, 'we've only just managed to seal the Mid Deck. The zoids could attack at any moment.' He shakes his head. 'And even if, by some miracle, you did make it into the Outer Hull, the zoids are in complete control up there. You wouldn't stand a chance. The humans they haven't exterminated have been enslaved.'

I nod, remembering the sight of those men, women and children who stumbled out of the container-pod as mindless human shields.

Cronos flexes his wings. 'And anyway, even if you did

manage to . . . York, are you listening to me? York?'

I look up. Truth is, I'm not. Caliph leaps down onto my shoulder and I stroke his head thoughtfully.

'I've had an idea,' I say.

# 46

I'm standing in the great atrium of the Sanctuary dome. It feels great to be back, even for this fleeting moment. The Sanctuary-dwellers and the genetically modified humans are now working together – although repairing and conserving the bio-zones of the Mid Deck has had to stop for the time being.

The atmosphere is every bit as tense as the atmosphere back in the underground laboratory. Everyone expects a zoid attack to be launched at any moment.

Every man, woman and child has been kitted out with protective gear. They're wearing urilium breastplates and visored helmets, elbow and knee hubs, and deflector shields as protection from laser fire. The adults are tooled up with weapons too; pulsers, stunners, gunkball launchers . . .

Having seen the upgraded killer zoids that came out of the transporters, I'm far from sure any of this will be enough to stop them. At least not for long.

My friend Travis is standing next to me. He is now

in charge of the Sanctuary. It's been good catching up with him. He's just shown me around, pointing out the changes that have taken place since I was last here. The sleep-pods which used to control everyone's thoughts have been disconnected. The visiglass walls and floor have been covered, offering privacy. The bloodthirsty 'mutant' holo-games have been erased. And in the refectory, real food has replaced the taste-pills.

Once gleaming and sterile, the place is now a bustling kitchen, pots bubbling on hobs, pans sizzling. And it smells amazing.

It smells like . . .

life.

'This plan of yours,' says Travis, looking me up and down, 'do you think it'll work, York?'

Belle appears, striding towards us from the armoury. I hardly recognize her.

I turn to Travis and swallow uneasily. 'It's got to work,' I tell him.

# 47

Dextra, Cronos and Travis stand, surrounded by Mid-Deckers and their droids. Belle and I look back at their worried faces as the doors of Transporter 1 close with an eerie clang.

We're on our own.

The inter-level transportation unit lurches into motion, a steady hum building as it gathers speed. In the corners of the huge container-pod are the shattered remains of the zoids knocked out in that first battle. But the parts are too damaged to be of use. As a scavenger, I can see that.

So much waste and destruction. So much pain and death. And all because of that tiny little bit of data that Belle managed to record and store in her chest panel; the tiny string of code that Marston deleted and now Belle must reinsert. Everything I've been through – the whole epic journey with Belle down through the layers of the Biosphere – and it all depends on this.

I turn and look at Belle. And she must see something in my expression, because she reaches out and takes me by the hand. And smiles.

'York,' she says softly, 'it's going to be all right.'

I want to believe her. Of course I do. But Belle's become so human, and this is just the sort of thing one human would say to another human to reassure them. Even if it wasn't true.

All too soon, the container-pod comes to a halt. There's a soft mechanical *dong* and the doors slide jerkily open. As we step outside, my breath catches in my throat . . .

I'm back in a world I recognize – the world I was born into, so different from the gleaming, well-ordered Biosphere of the past. We're at the edge of some dark and dirty tube-forest. Pipes, thick with centuries of dust, drip and hiss and hum. Parasitic plants have sunk their roots into tiny cracks and crevices, their rubbery leaves or feathery fronds hanging down around us. To our right the forest gives way to a broad plain dotted with flux stacks and power pylons. To our left is a tall cylindrical generator tower – out of action.

I turn to Belle. 'Which way?' I say.

'According to my schematics, the zoid central computer is located in Sector 4. That way,' she says, pointing. 'Past the sump reserves.'

I turn and look at the rows and rows of circular tanks laid out ahead of us, each one filled with pitch-black oil. They seem to go on forever.

Belle pauses. She stiffens, staring straight ahead, unblinking.

'Killer zoids,' she hisses out of the corner of her mouth. 'Three of them. Approaching from behind.'

I don't turn. Neither does she. Instead we both raise our arms slightly at our front, stiffen our leg movements and lurch slowly but steadily on towards the oil tanks.

I hear the zoids clomping towards us. Closer . . . Closer . . .

I fight the urge to break into a run. To conceal myself in some shadowy crevice and wait for them to pass. After all, it's what we humans have been doing for centuries. But I don't. Not this time.

This time I'm not human.

Out of the corner of my eye I can see Belle. She's dressed in faded rags – a torn tunic she picked up at the Sanctuary, a battered belt and scuffed boots. Me, I'm dressed the same. A worn flakcoat, one sleeve coming loose at the shoulder. A frayed shirt. Filthy breeches. The sole of one of my boots flaps as I shuffle forward.

Around both our necks, in stark contrast to the tatty clothing, are shiny urilium bands, each one studded with a row of flickering white lights. These are what the zoids lock on to now. I listen to the soft bleeping sound our control-collars are making, and hope the zoids' sensors are picking them up too.

The three zoids are right behind us now. I feel the ground tremble as their heavy footsteps land, one after the other. I smell the telltale whiff of hot wiring they give off.

Still lurching forward, I let my eyelids droop as I stare ahead unblinking. My mouth's dry with fear. But there's just enough moisture for me to send a glistening strand of drool dripping down from one corner of my mouth.

Blinking and buzzing, the zoids lumber past us. They're colossal, armoured and heavily weaponed. Their massive legs threaten to crush us at any moment.

Keep your nerve, I tell myself.

One after the other they stomp ahead, before veering off and heading towards the energy plains. I don't know where they're going. I don't care. They've identified the pair of us as brain-dead and harmless – and that's all that matters.

I wait until they disappear from view.

'It worked,' I whisper to Belle.

'It worked,' she whispers back.

We increase our speed as we keep on walking, but maintain the same rolling side-to-side lurch. And when, half an hour or so later, we approach a group of five sorry-looking humans stumbling towards us in the opposite direction, we pass by each other, our collars bleeping. They don't acknowledge us, and we don't acknowledge them.

We continue. The Outer Hull, I see, is more run-down and scuzzy than ever. Bits of it are completely devastated. Air ducts and ventilation units have been ransacked. Power stacks, generator towers, energy hubs – they've all been trashed. The zoids have used the parts to upgrade themselves, becoming bigger, stronger. More monstrous. On top of that, they've upgraded the simpler zoids, like tanglers and sluicers, leaving none to carry out essential maintenance.

As a result, everything's falling to bits. Much longer, and the whole place will grind to a complete halt. For humans at least. Maybe the zoids will be able to maintain the Biosphere, but only for themselves. They have no need of oxygen, warmth, a constant air pressure. But the surviving humans themselves are in a sorry state.

We keep coming to once-hidden Inposts that have been discovered by the zoids, then ransacked and destroyed. As for the humans who might once have lived in them, we don't come across a single one who hasn't had their mind drained.

I'm beginning to fear we're already too late.

'It's this way,' says Belle as we reach the end of the sump reserves.

We enter a broad area containing what look like storage pods and zigzag our way between the squat buildings. There's flaking white paint on the tarnished metal doors. Some are just numbers and letters that mean nothing to us. Some detail what has been stored inside. Twice Belle stops in front of a door, reads the sign, checks it against the coordinates she has stored and moves on. The third time, she turns to me.

'Here,' she says.

I frown. 'This is the zoid central computer?' I say.

'It is,' Belle tells me. 'At least,' she adds, 'according to the schematics Bronx gave me.'

I stare at the door. It's hard to believe. I assumed we would come to some vast computer complex, surrounded by energy shields and complete with banks of info-stacks, tech-decks and data-drives – as well as a small army of killer zoid guards. Instead I'm staring at a storage pod as squat and nondescript as all the others.

But then, with the human threat eliminated in the Outer Hull, the zoids have turned all their attention to conquering the Mid Deck. And whatever it is on the other side of this door, it's controlling their efforts.

Belle activates the control panel on the wall. The door slides open and we step inside.

The storage pod looked small from outside. Inside it's enormous. There's a ramp at the far end that leads underground, and Belle and I find ourselves looking down into a cavernous chamber that's chugging and humming and glowing with golden light.

'Any zoids?' I whisper to Belle.

She pauses, then shakes her head. 'None that I can detect.'

Keeping careful watch, we head down the gently sloping ramp. All around us vast banks of tech-stacks and data-modules are embedded in the walls, flashing and humming. At the bottom of the ramp we stop and look around. My heart's thumping. I turn to Belle again.

'Anything?'

She shakes her head, but pulls a pulser from inside her tattered jacket. I do the same.

The floor is completely covered with an intricate tracery of systems lights, communication conduits and energy power-lines.

'They're all leading in that direction,' Belle says, and

points across the floor to the very centre of the chamber, where they converge on a dark shape.

We're about to check it out when suddenly there's a blinding flash. I spin round.

'Belle!' I gasp.

She's down on her knees, her back arched. A crackling bolt of energy descending from the ceiling is pinning her to the floor.

'I'm being scanned . . .' she manages to tell me as her body convulses. 'York . . . you must save . . . the data . . . you must . . .'

She pulls a cutter from her belt and presses it into my trembling hand.

'It has detected me as a zoid . . .' She points to my control-collar. 'You are human,' she says. 'It thinks you are no threat . . . But it knows that I could access . . . the central computer . . . I . . . I can't hold it back much longer . . .'

Belle's body jolts and judders again and again as the energy beam grows in strength.

'Yo . . . ork,' she groans.

I look at the cutter in my hand, then back at Belle. I understand what she's asking me to do.

I am a scavenger. She is a zoid . . .

But she is my friend.

I can't . . .

'Do it, York . . .' Belle says, her voice barely a whisper. She's motionless now. Her body is rigid. Her eyes are closed. 'Do it . . .'

I know it can't hurt her, that she's a machine without pain sensors. But what will happen to her? I'm trembling as I take the cutter in my hand. Swiftly, carefully, I insert the blade and remove the chest panel. My hand is sticky with zoid-juice, my eyes blurry with tears.

A pulse of energy crackles across the surface of Belle's skin as she gives in to it. I watch, the panel clutched in my hands. Suddenly the energy bolt snaps off and Belle slumps face forward onto the floor.

She doesn't move again.

'Remove the unit for analysis,' says a voice.

I look round. 'You,' I breathe.

# 49

A Robotic-Assist Level Personal Help stands rooted at the centre of the chamber. A Mark 1. All the energy streams are converging at its stubby feet, which are embedded in the floor. As I approach it, the light catches on a long scratch and a small dent on the left of the robot's head.

It's Samuel Marston's personal help. The good robot that he turned bad.

I remember Sophie, the young bio-engineer who arrived in the medi-centre just after Marston was killed. She was so upset. Told the others to make sure they stored the mission commander's lifelong faithful servant away carefully . . .

They did that all right.

Centuries later, the robotic unit looks no different. Dumpy. Friendly-faced. Except now, thanks to the deleted piece of protocol, it has passed on the glitch – just as I saw happen in the store hangar – turning all of the robots bad. Then controlling them.

'Remove the unit for analysis,' it says again in that polite voice I have got to know so well.

Thanks to the bleeping collar, its sensors are telling it I am a human slave. Belle has not been so lucky. The collar couldn't disguise what she was. Not here in the zoid control computer.

I fight a wave of anger that rises up in me. I must stay calm. Stay focused.

For Belle.

'Show me your protocol access key,' I say calmly, repeating the words I heard Marston use back in the memory bank.

For a moment the little robot doesn't say anything, but the floor lights up and tracery glows all over the chamber. It recognizes the words and, despite the power of the zoid central computer, the robot at its centre is programmed to respond.

'My protocol access key is restricted, sir,' it says.

'Mission-commander override,' I say. 'Marston . . .' I pause. 'Double-helix eight.'

'Mission-commander override in need of dual-verification, sir,' Mark responds, just as I hoped.

'Dual-verification. Atherton . . .' I rack my brains. 'Double helix . . . four.'

'Override accepted,' it says.

The familiar glowing circular disc is projected in the air above it, a network of lights glowing on them. More discs appear. More and more. Until for a second time I'm staring at this hypnotic constellation of twinkling lights.

I raise the panel in my hands and it glows bright. A single line of dancing symbols hovers in the air.

It's the data-memory, ready to be re-uploaded.

I concentrate. The missing line of data has to be put back in exactly the right place. Without Belle, this isn't going to be easy. I scan the discs, willing myself to recognize the gap in the digital protocol they contain. But it's no good. There's simply too much data spinning past my eyes. But just then the panel emits a jolt of energy that makes my fingers tingle.

And there it is! The gap. On the disc just in front of me. I tilt the panel, and the line of data slips into place, glows brightly for an instant, then the disc goes spinning off to join the rest.

'Thank you, Belle,' I whisper.

'Protocol restored,' says a familiar voice, and a buzzing charge of energy pulses out from the robot and along the power cables. 'My name is . . . is . . . is . . .'

Then everything abruptly falls silent.

I turn to the little robot. If the protocol has been restored, then it should have become an obedient servant once more. But something has happened. The lights in its eyes have gone out. It isn't moving.

Perhaps the power surge was too much for it. Perhaps something has shorted. Or perhaps, with the protocol back in place, Mark had a moment of terrible knowledge of what it did to humanity and has deactivated itself again.

Whatever, it – he – is broken.

I stand looking at him. I want

to see his large eyes glowing red once more, rather than those two evil-looking yellow dots. I want to hear his friendly voice reassuring me that everything is all right now. But Mark is gone. Forever.

Then I remember . . .

I reach into my pocket. Is it still there? Yes. My fingers close around a small tube of metal – the silver interface unit with the simple memory chip embedded in it, that I recovered when a faithful personal help robot, just like Mark, sacrificed himself to save my life.

I click open the small panel in the robot's chest and remove the interface unit. It's blackened and smoking, and I toss it away. I insert the silver unit in its place, my fingers trembling, then press the button at the back.

The little robot gives a start and begins to hum. The head jerks up. The big red shining eyes switch on. The dumpy body swivels round to face me.

'My name is Ralph,' he says. 'How may I serve you?'

The lights are on. The air smells fresh. Pipes and tubes buzz and hum and slosh with the heat, oxygen, water, power and all the rest passing through them. On the far side of the sump reserves, a small group of individuals is busy fixing a power pylon.

They're a mismatched bunch. There's a stonking great zoid from the Outer Hull, two spindle-legged droids from the Mid Deck and four humans. While the zoid – or rather the now obedient robot – holds the pylon above the ground, the droids reconnect the cables; then the humans – two men and two women – move from power unit to power unit, repairing burned-out stagger-fuses, replacing transistors and capacitors and resetting volt-lapsers and timer-switches.

At the foot of a broken generator tower I pass a humongous zoid that, with the help of two others, is dismantling itself for parts. Further on, robots and humans are seeing to a sparking power-hub.

'Robots and humans,' I say softly, 'working as a team.'

Robots are following their complete protocol once

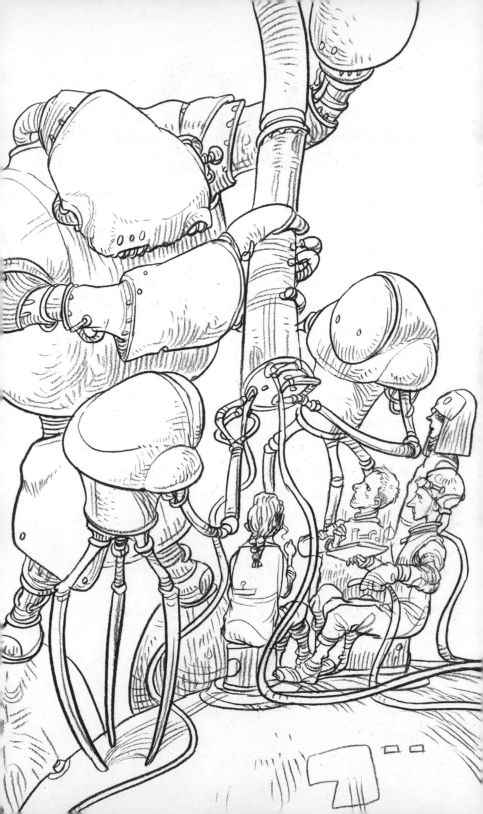

more – to serve both the Biosphere *and* humans. To sum it up, the robot rebellion is over.

I step into an elevator, which whirrs into action. As I rise up through the levels, I look out of the visiglass window at the atrium, and once again my gaze settles upon the thousand-year-old oak tree in the grow-trough at its centre.

I know all about deciduous trees and how they shed their leaves once a year. But it's a shock to see the ancient tree looking dead. Except . . .

I press my face to the visiglass for a better look. And, yes, I was right. Every brown stick-like twig is tipped with the green of new shoots. I smile to myself. It seems like a good omen.

At the top level, the elevator comes to a halt. I step out, make my way along the corridor to the viewing deck. The doors glide open – and my jaw drops.

The place is packed.

There are men, women and children. Modified and unmodified. Most of them I don't know. Some of them I do. Travis, Dextra and Cronos. Lina and Dek – and the small, furry critter sitting on his shoulder, that suddenly lets out a high-pitched screech and comes scampering towards me.

'Caliph!' I'm grinning from ear to ear as he scampers up my arm, crouches down on my shoulder

and starts licking my ear.

'Greetwell, York.'

I look round to see that, in the midst of the great crowd of people, are two mind-tombs. The glowing faces of the Half-Lifes within them are smiling warmly.

'Bronx,' I say. 'Atherton.'

'I'm glad you could join us, York,' Bronx tells me. 'You need to see this.'

People are smiling at me, congratulating me, patting me on the back. Above us, the tinted visiglass is fading to reveal the view outside the Biosphere.

When I was last here, I also looked out. It was the first time I'd ever seen anything beyond the Biosphere. Asteroids. Planets. Suns. A meteor storm. Entire constellations of stars passing us as we hurtled through space. Now a different scene greets me . . .

A planet.

It's blue and green, with oceans of water and vast continents. There are two large white patches, one at either side of the great sphere, which I guess must be polar ice, and ribbons of white cloud that swirl over parts of the surface. Half of the planet is in darkness, and when I crane my neck I see, far to my right, the yellow sun that this world is orbiting.

Dek turns to me and grins. Lina gives me a hug and Travis slaps me on the back. Caliph purrs in my ear.

I look at the planet, tears welling in my eyes. Tears of happiness. We've travelled halfway across the universe to find it. Now that search is over.

And me? I've been a scavenger all my life. With humans and robots working together once more, that life

is over. But a new one is about to start.

'You did it, York.'

I turn to see Belle standing at my side. Not only has she been repaired, but she looks better than ever.

'*We* did it,' I tell her. 'You and me, Belle, together.'

*The Beginning*

# SCAVENGER ZOID

## PAUL STEWART    CHRIS RIDDELL

### A SPACESHIP THE SIZE OF A CONTINENT DRIFTS THROUGH SPACE ON ITS JOURNEY TO FIND A NEW EARTH.

Originally created to serve the human passengers, the high-tech robots on-board the spaceship rebelled and became powerful zoids, wiping out most of the crew. Now the few remaining humans are hunted like vermin and hiding in the dark.

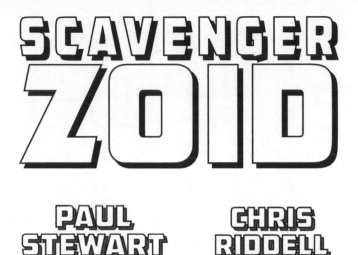

But one scavenger refuses to hide. Instead York spends his days tracking down zoids and destroying them. But the zoids are becoming more dangerous by the day. And now the fate of his people is in York's hands . . .

# SCAVENGER CHAOS ZONE

## PAUL STEWART

## CHRIS RIDDELL

**WHEN A MASSIVE SPACESHIP SET OUT ON A MISSION TO FIND NEW EARTH, THE ROBOTS ON-BOARD REBELLED. NOW ONLY A FEW HUMANS REMAIN, HUNTED AND AFRAID . . .**

But York is not afraid. He is a scavenger on a mission – a mission to fight back. In a world of tropical rainforests and a huge ocean aquarium, where the people, plants and animals are mutating in strange and disturbing ways, nothing and no one are ever as they seem.

With the fate of his people in his hands and the world in chaos, who can York trust?